Carl B. Yoke

the
DARK ONE COMES
and
the BOOK of the
HORNED GOD
THE MICHAEL HOLLAND STORIES II

outskirts
press

Outskirts Press, Inc.
http://www.outskirtspress.com

ISBN: 978-1-9772-0940-5

Cover Image by Brian Wootan

Outskirts Press and the "OP" logo are trademarks belonging to Outskirts Press, Inc.

PRINTED IN THE UNITED STATES OF AMERICA

With Love to Sherry
& Andrea

TA –

   Hope your cat is better by now...
Sebastian (?)
    This is my latest. Enjoy the read.
     Carl.
Talk by phone this coming Sunday (?)

     Carl

Acknowledgements

Roger Zelazny, my very best friend; we wrote stories together; Tom Auld, a friend and watercolorist who I've talked to endlessly about my stories; Linda Ellis, for her excellent, recent advice; Mary Turzillo, who urged me to try to publish my stories; and to all my teachers who encouraged my writing through the years.

The Dark One Comes

Thena sat in her Camaro outside of Raven's house on Canyon Drive and waited for her friend's return. Her anxiety grew with each passing moment, and time dragged by. She had been waiting more than an hour already. And as she watched the clouds mass over the city, it seemed twilight, and she knew that it was going to snow again.

"Damn," she whispered to no one in particular. "Where can she be?"

She had tried to call before she left her apartment in Denver, but there was no answer. In fact, she had tried several times with no success, both her landline and her cell. Thena was nearly in panic when she finally hopped into her car and drove to Boulder. Her heart was beating rapidly, her breath came in short gasps, and she was sweating heavily, despite the fact that the outside temperature was in the mid-twenties.

She had momentarily considered driving to the University to talk to Professor Burnes, but Raven had told her that in spite of his interest he didn't really believe in the paranormal. Raven, at least, knew that some parts of it were real, and she knew that there were beings who could not be explained away without fair consideration.

She had also tried to call Marcus, but no one was answering there either. What was going on she wondered? It had seemed like a long time since either of them had talked with him. Thena had even called the Classics Department of Baldwin Wallace and the secretary told her that he had taken an unexpected leave of absence … ostensibly because of a house fire in Gates Mills. What could that mean, she wondered? And why had he not called her? Had something happened to him? And if it had, would anyone even have notified her? Sylvia was out of the country, but Maddie, the housekeeper, knew how to reach her. At least she could have called *The Gazette*, and left a message. But she had received no communication at all.

The thought that Sylvia was missing in Turkey chilled her. Even though she came along after Thena had gone to college, she was like a mother to her.

Her mind drifted.

She felt jealous when she thought about that gypsy woman Michael had formed an unnatural attachment for. Lilly was her name. Thena had been aware of a woman named Lilly when she spent a semester in Paris … very beautiful, but very dark. And, she hung around with a bunch of gypsies. The rumor was that she was an accomplished thief. She remembered a myth that Marcus used to tell about a band of gypsies that tried to help Jesus when he was on his way to the cross, and how to reward them he told them it was okay to steal. Something in the narrative did not quite add up, but Marcus could provide no other explanation. Yes, she knew quite well that Lilly had a hold over Michael, but she was convinced that neither Lilly or her cousins had anything to do with Michael becoming a rider on that horse in the snow storm. Such antics, she reasoned, were quite beyond them. Fitting a gypsy into that supernatural scenario made no sense at all even though it was clear to her that Lilly was much more than what she seemed.

She remembered hearing Al Wilson's song, "The Snake" on an oldies radio station out of Denver as she drove to Boulder. She was what she was. But Michael had found that out in his relationship with her. He struggled, but he could not break free of her. And she didn't understand what he saw in her. Anyway, the gypsy made no secret about who she was.

Thena suddenly felt powerless, alone, and betrayed.

Then, as the sun began to disappear beyond the mountains, and she felt that she was about to cry, she recovered her composure. She took a sip from a thermos of hot coffee which she was now grateful that she had taken time to pour and heat before she started the trip.

She knew that she was super-smart, but she had always let her emotions interfere with her thinking. She was a master problem solver. And here she was facing one hell of a problem.

She needed to think, to reason her way through the maze. If Michael had been atomized and sucked into the painting, then there had to be a way to reverse the process. She had resources at her disposal – money and, more importantly, people who might have ideas about how to reverse the process. What she needed to do was break free of her emotions and marshal her assets. She knew it could be done. After all, Lucifer had gotten down from a cross and walked out of the Cleveland Art Museum.

She was reviewing her options when her phone rang.

She looked down at the caller ID and hope flashed through her. It was Marcus.

"Marcus," she began, "Thank God! I thought something awful had happened to you."

"Not yet," he replied, "but not because they haven't tried."

"Who?" she asked puzzled.

"Don't know. And I don't know if someone is actually trying to kill me or just scare me. If the later, then they have succeeded. And," he added, "I can't figure out why."

"Maybe I can help," she offered. "Some very strange things have been happening here. And I think they're all connected … though I can't figure out how yet."

"We need to talk," he said, "and phones aren't entirely safe. We need to talk face to face. Right away."

"But I'm in Colorado," she started to protest. "And I can't get to you …."

"It's okay. I can't say exactly where I am. It wouldn't be safe, but I've got an idea. You remember where you and Michael used to eat lunch when you had to go downtown, together?" He stressed the together.

"Of course!"

"Find the one closest to your apartment in Denver. I'll meet you there at noon tomorrow."

"Okay, but …."

"Noon tomorrow," he repeated. "Got to hang up. Been on this phone too long already. Remember, where you guys used to stop to eat."

He hung up.

She was puzzled. She hadn't even had an opportunity to tell him about Michael's predicament. She hadn't been able to get a word in edgewise.

But she didn't have much time to think about it more because Raven's old, silver Audi pulled into the driveway a few moments later.

———◈———

"I'm sorry you had to wait," began Raven, "but I had to get some information from members of my coven."

"No problem," said Thena, trying to maintain her composure.

"Come on, I'll get you a drink. I need one. What would you like?"

"Tanqueray and tonic, or some white wine."

"Tanqueray and tonic, then. That'll suit me too."

She rose and began to head to the kitchen. "It'll just take me a few minutes."

Thena shrugged, but was about to burst with anxiety.

"I didn't know how to deal with her," she heard coming from the kitchen. "So, I canvassed my colleagues for advice, just to see if they knew anything."

"What did they tell you?" asked Thena, anxious to tell her about what had happened to Michael, but aware of how distressed Raven was.

She gestured nothing. "Truth is none of us, me included, has had any experience with a being like her." Raven took the pitcher, got two glasses out of the cupboard, and motioned Thena back into the living room, where both women sat down.

"I turned off my phones and answering machine. I was afraid she'd track me down. I needed time to figure out some way to handle her."

"Who is she? Who are you talking about?" asked Thena while Raven sipped her drink.

"Oh!" said Raven. "I forgot to tell you who I was complaining about. Morgan Le Fey was how she identified herself."

"Morgan!" said Thena surprised. "My God. What did she want?"

"My *Book of Shadows*. I'm sorry. I just needed some time," explained Raven, "to figure things out."

Thena nodded and then replied, "so what happened?"

Raven explained how she changed shapes and threatened her. Then she found the book on her own and took off with it. "I was literally paralyzed with fear. After she got it, she disappeared. I thought I would talk to my coven members to see if any of them had had any contact with shape changers before."

"I'm sorry," apologized Thena. "I may have put her on to you accidently. Believe me, I didn't mean to."

"It's okay. And I'm glad you are here. The company helps me calm down."

Raven sighed periodically while they sipped their drinks.

"Look," began Thena, "I don't want to intrude. You're clearly upset."

"It's okay. I just need some time to deal with it."

"Are you okay now ... because if you are, I've got a doozy of a problem that I've got to talk to someone about."

Raven nodded okay.

Thena gathered herself and then launched into what happened to Michael.

"Wow!" said Raven, pausing for what seemed a very long time. She sipped her drink. Finally, she spoke. "Welcome to the world of weird. You do have a problem ... one I've never encountered before. Can I help you? Is there anything I can do?"

"Well," Thena began, "I don't think any normal person can explain what happened to Michael. You remember the guy who we told you about that dragged his cross down the steps of the Cleveland Art Museum?"

Raven nodded. "Yes. What about him?"

"Well," continued Thena, "he had apparently been on the cross for centuries, but he never told us how he happened to get there."

Raven listened attentively, then rose, took Thena's glass, and went back into the kitchen. She returned a few moments later. "I'm not ignoring you," she said. "I'm actually thinking about the problem."

"Well, the important thing is that he somehow got out of the painting and off the cross. Michael and I believed his story, as wild as it seems. So, I need to find a way to get Michael out of another painting called *Astride A Horse of Winter* without harming him or changing him. I spent a couple of hours in the car waiting for you to return and thinking, and I figure the only person who can help us is Hannah Fox. Unfortunately, she's in the sprite trap. I know you told me how to get her back out, but how do we control her once we do?"

Raven thought about what Thena had said for a few moments then, finally spoke. "What do you think she might want?" she asked.

"The only thing I can think of is another painting, called *The Disobedient*, that Michael bought in a gallery in Fort Collins. He followed Morgan up there the evening that we trapped Fox in the sprite trap by mistake. He happened to see her in the gallery looking at the painting for a long time. He talked to the owner, a man named Merchant, about her and he told Michael that she came there often to look at it. But when he offered her a deal to buy it, she said that it was safer where it was. In other words, she turned him down."

"I get it," said Raven. "Her fascination with the picture is why you think it's important to her."

"Exactly!"

"So, let me see if I understand this right. You want to get her out of the trap and trade that picture for her help."

"Yeah. I'll use the picture for bait. I won't give it to her until I'm satisfied that she's given me all she knows."

"But she's a trickster," cautioned Raven. "Who knows if she'll tell you the truth."

Thena shrugged. "Maybe, maybe not. Maybe, she'll just be so grateful to be out of the trap that she'll help me. After all, wouldn't her body just start to break down, after a while, into her essential atoms and then eventually be whisked to some limbo?"

"I don't know. Seems logical."

"It's worth a try."

Both women were quiet while they thought the situation over.

Finally, Raven spoke, "when do you want to release her?" she asked.

"A couple of days. I've got other things I need to attend to first. Like I want to remove *The Disobedient* painting from my apartment … put it into a safe place."

Raven nodded that she understood. "All right, let me know when and where you want to do this."

⸺⸻◈⸻⸺

She knew what Marcus meant because she and Michael had often grabbed food at a Pizza Hut on Euclid Avenue, but she was sure that he wouldn't be there now. Even though it was only a few blocks from her apartment. So, she was pleasantly surprised when she entered and spotted him sitting by himself in a dark corner away from the windows.

He waved her over. She returned the wave and pointed to herself, then the salad bar. She then gathered up a plate, filled it and carried it to the table.

He rose, smiled broadly, and gave her a bear hug.

When he released her, she said, "I'm glad, I was really worried about you when I couldn't reach you."

"I've been in Denver for a while. I've been trying to stay close to you and at the same time lay low. I think someone has been following me. I'm not sure they mean to harm me, but you can't take chances. Everything that's happened is kind of ambiguous."

"I don't understand. Like what?" she said.

He drew a deep sigh. "Well, the brake line started leaking on my car. If I hadn't taken it in for service, the fluid might have run out entirely. And my office at the University was carefully gone through, as was my house in Gates Mills, even while Maddie was there. All this happened after I came back from Rome. I called the police in each instance, but they could find no evidence of an intruder, and since no crime was committed, they could do nothing. Then shots were fired as I was driving along that shattered my rear window on the driver's side. They weren't close to hitting me, but no one else was around, so, someone was warning me, but I don't know who and

I don't know why. This prompted me to take a medical leave from BW. I was sure my computer was hacked and I think my phone was tapped. But I don't know enough about the technology to prove any of it. And," he added, "there was the fire. The fire department thought it might have happened because of a flue that wasn't open, but I always open it when I light a fire. It's like part of my routine."

"Curious. What do you think whoever is doing this wants from you?"

He shrugged.

"But Sylvia told me a few days ago …"

"Is she back?" interrupted Thena.

"Yeah. I was going to get into that in a few minutes. Now, she's keeping a low profile just like me."

"What happened to her?" asked Thena.

"Kidnapped. Held for a couple of days and warned about continuing to look into the activities of several secret groups with strange names."

"Like what?"

"Sons of Light, Keepers of the Sun, the Protectors of the Moon, Daughters of God and so on. She wasn't investigating any of them. In fact, she'd never even heard of any of them. They were, she believes, alchemists, neo-alchemists, neo-apothecaries, and other secret societies. So, she promised that she wouldn't look into the affairs of a half dozen or so groups, and they let her go."

"But no torture, right?"

"Right. But they gave her some kind of drugs, maybe LSD. She was in a world of her own for a few days – hallucinations. Devils, imps, angels, vampires, werewolves, golems, and fairy tale creatures. Some good, some bad. Anyway, it worked on her. She won't be helping us openly anymore. She'll still help us, but it won't be so open."

"Well, she wasn't doing that much for us. I'm just happy she's okay. I missed her something awful."

"One more thing. They had a lot of questions about Michael. They didn't believe he could have gotten rid of that creature calling himself Lucifer. It bothered them a great deal. They seemed to think he had some sort of special powers. But they can't figure out who he is or what his powers can be."

She pouted, "I was there too, you know!"

"So, you've told me. But they seemed to have little respect for women. They figured you were just doing what he told you to."

"Well damn them!" she exclaimed almost in a whisper.

"It's a man's world … as it has so often been."

That seemed to shut down the conversation.

"You seemed almost panicky when I talked to you on the phone. What's wrong?"

She looked down at her feet and sighed.

"I have something I need to give you – for safe keeping. I need for you to take it, and I can't really explain it adequately. I need to show you. It's in my car."

"Okay," he said. "When we finish eating, we can go see it."

They finished quickly and went out to the car. She directed him to the trunk which she opened. In it were two paintings covered by clean tarps.

"You need to keep these for me … somewhere safe, until I call you. I don't want to know where you put them. Just to be cautious."

She pulled the tarp off of the *Astride a Horse of Winter* picture and pointed to it.

"This is a valuable painting. And I need to keep it safe."

"Okay," he said. "How much is it worth? And how did you come by it?"

"I purchased this painting for Michael at an auction in Montreal. It's not especially valuable in a monetary sense, but look there," she said, pointing down at the picture of the rider on the horse.

"It looks just like Michael. A coincidence?"

"It doesn't just look like him, it is him," she said with tears beginning to fill her eyes.

"Can't be," he said, "That's not possible."

"Yes, it is. I stood and watched him dissolve into atoms, then flow into the paint, and solidify in that figure."

"But that makes no sense," he protested. "It's against the laws of physics."

"Think about it," she said with a slight smile. "What happens to our bodies when we die."

"Is that a hypothetical question?"

"No, no. It's a scientific question." Without waiting for an answer, she provided one herself. "They decompose ... break down into atoms which flow into other things ..."

He frowned, scratched his head.

"It's him," she assured. "I saw it happen."

"Is he dead then?"

"I don't think so, but I really don't know. I think it's more like being imprisoned. Remember when we told you about the figure on the cross in Grunwald's panel ... him hauling it down the steps of the Art Museum and dragging it half way around Wade Lagoon?"

"I do," he replied.

"But why him? And how do we get him back?" He repeated his question.

"I don't know. But I'm working on an idea. I have a friend, a neo-apothecary, named Raven, whose house was just invaded by Morgan Le Fey. She terrorized my friend and took her *Book of Shadows*. But that's a story for another time. Raven is quite knowledgeable. She knows some of what we need to do. And I've got Le Fey's sister in a sprite trap. Her name is Hannah Fox, everyone usually calls her Fox but she sometimes goes by the nickname Kit. We believe she is a trickster ... at least she's one of those extradimensional creatures that have been labeled tricksters in various world mythologies."

She put her hand into her bag, pulled out the bottle with Fox in it, and handed it to him. He examined it carefully.

"Well, I trapped her by mistake and we never completed the process of disposing of her by burying the bottle which, I've been told, would result in her dissolution. Michael thought she could be useful to us … before he got absorbed into the painting. First, we would have to get her back out of the trap and control her. On a hunch, Michael followed Le Fey to Fort Collins and bought that other picture there. Le Fey was looking for Fox and lead Michael to the painting"

She pointed to the other picture which was still under the tarp. Marcus pulled the tarp off and examined it. "*The Disobedient,*" he whispered under his breath.

"You know it?"

He shook his head. "Not really, but I've heard it mentioned."

"Michael found out that Fox was fascinated by it, went to the gallery a couple of times a year to look at it. When he asked about the picture's history, the owner, a man named Merchant, told him that when he offered to sell it to Fox for a relatively cheap price, she made a curious remark, that it would probably be safer where it was."

"What do you two make of all this?"

"Well, I think we can bribe Fox with it. At first, we thought we could get her to help us find Le Fey, who, by the way, now has both the Moon sign, the Venus, and the Sun sign, the Helix, and has disappeared. But now, I would like Fox to help me get Michael out of the painting. I need him back. And, I don't know what prolonged imprisonment might do to him."

Marcus scratched his head slightly as he puzzled over the problem. "Maybe dissolution is built into the capturing spell, a kind of terminus of sorts."

"Maybe," she agreed. "And I assume that whoever prepared the spell in the canvas could make it produce whatever result he had in mind."

"So," said Marcus, "what's the plan?"

"Raven and I are meeting tomorrow to get Fox out of the sprite trap. Then, we'll use her to get Michael out of the painting."

"Do you want me to come along?" he asked.

"No," she answered. "I think it best if you take the two pictures away from here and stash them some place safe."

He nodded okay.

"I don't want to know where you put them, or where you are. I just want to know how to reach you if this works."

"Good. I'll leave you the number of my answering service."

He smiled at her.

"As a caution, I'm going to keep moving. But I won't be hard to reach."

She nodded that she understood.

"By the way," he began as he picked up the pictures, one under each arm and headed for his car. "The word disobedient had a broader meaning for the Old Testament fathers, more than just not obeying. It implied active and violent rebellion against authority."

"Didn't know that," she said. "Do you think the figure in that picture is rebelling?"

He shrugged.

⌐⫷⬤⫸⌐

He watched for her to leave her apartment. Then, he parked his rented Camry on a side street a block away and walked back to her building. He knew she had the *Astride a Horse of Winter* painting from the tap he had placed on her phone, and he desperately wanted to get it and fix the spell before Pico or one of the other Sons of

Light found out that he had cast one on it … one he badly regretted. He meant to get back to it at the auction house in Montreal before the picture was sold and go over it just once more, to be sure he cast it right. But he got caught in traffic and when he finally returned the auction was over.

He went up the stairs to the second floor and stared briefly at the number to be sure he had the right one. Then he began a series of hand motions that he believed would unlock the door with what he thought was the appropriate spell.

But it failed. Nothing happened. He tried the knob, but the door was still locked. He jiggled the knob. Frustrated, he tried the spell again. Still nothing. He jiggled the handle again angrily.

He wanted that picture, the one that Holland had accidently been drawn into. He needed to figure out what he had done wrong and fix it before one of the Sons caught on. Maybe it was his hand motions. His bad hand had caused him problems before.

"Hey there!" came a voice from behind him. "What are you doing?"

He turned. A man about sixty, wearing jeans and a red and blue plaid, long sleeved shirt stood a few feet away at the bottom of the stairs coming down from the third floor.

"Hi," Crow began, thinking quickly. "I'm trying to get in to this apartment. This is Athena Thompkins apartment, isn't it?"

The man eyed him suspiciously.

"Yeah."

"Look," Crow continued. "I'm her cousin from San Francisco, here in Denver to attend a conference on Rogue Stars, and she told me I could bunk at her place for a few nights. But," he hurried right on, "she didn't send me a key … unless she left it with you. You're the super, aren't you?"

The old man nodded. "Yeah. I'm Wiggins. But she didn't leave a key with me."

Crow smiled broadly, walked forward, hand extended. He shook Wiggins' hand.

"You don't know where she is, do you? Maybe I could call her and let her know that I'm locked out. Or, I have another idea. Do you have a master key?" he asked.

The old man nodded yes.

"I hate to ask but could you just unlock the door and let me in? All my stuff … conference material and notebooks, are down in my car. And frankly, I want to put it inside and grab a nap before she comes home and wants to chat about what's going on with my side of the family. You know how women go on."

"Okay, I'll let you in," Wiggins agreed with a slight smile.

Thank goodness for charm, quick thinking and a gift for gab thought Crow. Wiggins hauled a large ring of keys from his pocket, searched for the right one and unlocked the door.

Crow searched the apartment for several minutes for the picture, but found nothing. He was careful, so she wouldn't catch on. He would have to go back to the phone tap and search for more information.

———◦《◎》◦———

That evening they sat on the floor with the sprite trap between them. The sun was setting and it peaked at the pulled blind with its red glow. They had created a pentagram with baking soda, placed a red candle at each angle of the pentagram, ten in all, and set some sweet grass burning on a small grill in the center. Each had a glass of Riesling and were sipping it.

"Are we ready?" asked Thena cautiously.

"The question is whether you are," said Raven. "Remember, you captured her. You have to say the spell in reverse to release her. At least that's what I think has to happen. Remember, none of us has ever released a sprite before." She hesitated for a few long seconds, then added, "We may as well go ahead and try it."

"And you'll be holding the red cord, right?"

Raven nodded.

"Then, we'll wrap her loosely in more red cord."

"Of course. Got it in hand."

"Okay then, here I go," she said as she pushed a sharp knife down the sides of the cork to free it up and pulled on the red string which had been tucked under it. Raven took the string in her left hand, carefully shifting the rest of the red string to her right. And Thena began to recite the sealing spell backward.

Thread, untie this sprit
Untangle her from the bone
Let not a piece
However small remain.
Ka!

They heard moaning and there was a sudden, very loud rushing sound coming from the bottle. After a few moments, there was a loud whoosh and a female figure began to form in front of them. Gradually, she solidified and Raven wrapped the red string around and around her. But it was not tight and did not restrict her movements. As she drifted toward the candles, she flinched, as if she had been burned, and glided back toward the center of the pentagram.

Raven practiced controlling her by pulling the string first left, then right.

Finally, Fox began to focus. "Thank you for freeing me. I owe you a lot."

"Just like getting a genie from a lamp," whispered Raven.

Thena smiled at her, then said, "We're just happy to have you back."

Fox stared at her for a few moments before recognition dawned. "I don't know who your friend is, but you … I recognize you from the auction in Montreal. And I also remember seeing you in Mexico."

"Right … on both occasions. And, I hate to admit it, but I was the one who trapped you in the bottle."

Fox looked mystified.

But Thena went right on. "I'm sorry," she began, "it was a case of mistaken identity. Michael, that's my fiancé, and I meant the trap for Morgan Le Fey."

"My sister!" she said shocked. "Why would you want her?"

"Because she now has both the Venus and the Helix, and we're afraid of what she might try to do with both of the icons in her control."

"I've got a terrible headache," said Fox. "Do either of you have some aspirin or Aleve?"

Raven nodded yes, handed the end of the red cord to Thena, and went into the kitchen. When she returned, she had two Bayer's and a full glass of water. She handed both of them to Fox who slapped the aspirin into her mouth and drank the whole glass of water.

"Well," she began at last. "One thing I've learned about being dispersed is it makes you thirsty. I wonder what beings, who are in traps a lot longer than I was, do," she added softly.

"Maybe, it affects each individual differently," said Thena.

"Well, thank you two for releasing me, but you've got to realize I can't grant you three wishes … or is it five? I don't have that ability. That's in fairy tales."

"We weren't looking for wishes," said Thena.

"Or treasure," added Raven.

"You don't seem to understand. It's not you that I was after. It was Le Fey. We were afraid of what she might try now that she has both of the icons," explained Thena.

"And well you should be," said Fox after a while. "One of her goals is power. She would love to dominate this world, this plane. There are beings from other planes here too, some more powerful than we are, who have similar goals. Lucifer, for example, was among them, and Azazal, and Belial. There are two groups on this plane dedicated to maintaining the balance, to keeping it free from interference. They want the unfettered flow of nature in this world."

Thena and Raven nodded knowingly as Fox went on and on. Finally, she stopped and asked, "Why did you two get me back out of the trap. It seems suspicious, if you truly know what I'm capable of."

"It would have been nice if you had given me wishes, but I understand that you can't. I was not expecting wishes, I was hoping" – she stressed the word hoping – "that you would help us."

"What can I possibly do for you?" asked Fox, surprised.

"You have information, you know your sister Morgan, and you know the dangers involved. We have to stop her."

"Oh," began Fox, "having the icons won't make her act soon."

"Why is that?" asked Raven.

Fox smiled slightly. "Because she has no idea of what they can actually do, and she doesn't know how to use them."

"Then, why steal them?" asked Thena.

"Well, frankly, a person has to take advantage of any opportunity she gets."

"So, you're saying that they were available?" asked Raven.

"More or less," replied Fox.

"How is she going to learn to use them?" asked Thena.

"She's probably going to find Dreaming Woman and ask for her help. Maybe she can find her, and maybe Dreaming Woman will actually help her. Then, you've got to ask yourself why would she."

"A bribe maybe," offered Thena.

"Who is this Dreaming Woman?" asked Raven.

"Ah, a being like Morgan and me from another dimension who has somehow become identified with the mythical Navajo woman Suisstanaka. The story goes that she can will things into being just by thinking of them. Of course, that is just myth, stories that build up around a being that may or may not be true. A bribe might work on her, if you can find something that she really wants. But, if she really can will things into being by just thinking about them, then no one can bribe her."

"I was going to bribe you," said Thena softly, "if letting you out of the trap wasn't enough to secure your help."

"And what could you offer me?" asked Fox with a slight chuckle.

"Well, Michael bought an oil painting in a gallery in Ft. Collins entitled *The Disobedient* that we thought you might be interested in."

Fox cringed noticeably.

Thena continued, "He followed Morgan to Ft. Collins when she went looking for you, saw you eyeing the painting in fascination, and bought it from a shop owner named Merchant on a hunch. He thought you might be able to help us, which is why we didn't complete the sprite trap by burying the bottle. Merchant told him how you often came to the gallery to look at it but wouldn't buy it because you felt it was safer where it was. Why is that?"

"I could just take it from you, if I chose," said Fox.

"No," replied Thena, "you couldn't."

"Really? And why not."

"Because I don't actually have access to it. In fact, I don't even know where it is."

"Oh!" said Fox, her voice betraying her disappointment. She huffed and thought about the offer for a while, then, "I would have preferred that it remained obscure in the little gallery in Old Town ... but since it's no longer there, I guess I have to protect it myself."

"I don't know what your connection is to the painting," said Thena, "but I can guess. The person being carried away by the warrior angels in the picture is very important to you."

"Very perceptive," said Fox. "He was once my lover ... but he was very independent minded and didn't like to be told what to do or what to think. And he was hot headed, angry all the time."

"So, he was punished for it."

"Yes."

"A rebel?" asked Raven.

"Yes," said Fox, "a rebel. Exactly. He was punished by one of the Sons of Light. Daniel thought he needed to be taught a lesson."

"Daniel? Who is that?" asked Thena.

"He's the current head of their group. Has been for a long time."

"So, why did you want to keep the painting safe?" asked Thena.

Fox sighed deeply, then said, "There are those beings in the protecting groups who feel that the man being carried away, Wolf, was getting off too easily. And if they knew where the picture was, they might add to his punishment somehow."

"But what did he do specifically?" asked Thena.

Fox forced a pained smile. "I only know what he told me. He said he dispersed someone in a moment of anger, someone he obviously shouldn't have." She shrugged, "I don't know any more about it. He's been in the painting ever since."

"And what would you do to get him out of the painting?" asked Thena.

Fox sighed again and pursed her lips. "Almost anything ... within reason."

"Then you'll help me with Dreaming Woman?"

Fox nodded yes.

"We do get lonesome a lot. Maybe love would entice Dreaming Woman … or at least companionship."

"Good idea. If she doesn't have someone, maybe we can persuade her. So," said Thena, "if you give me your promise, I'll set you free."

Fox nodded. And she dropped the red cord that had been binding Fox.

Crow picked up his cell phone and dialed Thena's number. It was one of the one's he had tapped. Then, he listened to what the machine had recorded. He heard her ask Professor Allensworth to bring the paintings to San Marcos. The professor said that it would be a few days because he had to recover them, but that he would call her again and let her know when he left Denver.

Crow smiled to himself. Not one but two paintings. He knew about the Rider picture, but he wondered what the other oil was. His curiosity was piqued. After some thought, he knew that he had to arrange two things. First, he needed a couple of Basque thieves from Idaho and second, he had to get a small amount of ketamine, to knock them out. He didn't want to have sex with the women. He just wanted to put fear into them.

He knew that if they were always looking over their shoulders, they would make mistakes.

The next evening, late, he drove north to Ft. Collins and found the man on the corner of University Boulevard and Second Street. After he parked, he approached him on foot.

"You Dobler," he asked.

"Depends" was the reply.

"I'm not a cop. Just looking for a good time."

"I don't know you," said Dobler. "Got ID?"

Crow hauled out his driver's license and handed it to Dobler.

"Okay," said the man as he edged back into the doorway and handed the license back to Crow. "What can I do for you?"

"I need some ketamine," said Crow.

Dobler shook his head. "What makes you think I can get that for you?"

"Reputation. I asked around … some of my college friends."

"You look kind of old for a college kid. How do I know you're not a cop?"

"You don't," replied Crow. "But I've got a Ben Franklin here to convince you."

"Only one?"

"You want two?"

Dobler smiled back at him.

"I'll go another fifty … but that's it. Otherwise, I'll look for someone else."

"Okay, okay. Don't get feisty. How, by the way, did you really know about me?"

"Everyone knows about you. As I said before, reputation."

"How did you know where to find me?"

"The police scanner mentions several places you might be. I just kept trying them until I found you."

Dobler was wearing a worn, blue pea coat and jeans, and he had a day's growth of beard.

He sighed. "Okay. Pill, liquid, or powder?"

"I guess powder. It seems to me it would be easiest to use."

Dobler reached into an inside coat pocket and pulled out a small, silver packet.

"Looks like a condom," said Crow casually.

"Would not know," said Dobler, "never use them myself. They cut down on the feel." He laughed.

Still smiling, he handed the packet to Crow. "Let's see your money."

Crow hauled out the money and handed it to him.

"You know what to do Noreen?"

She shook her head yes.

"Give each of them 30 milligrams. I want them out for a while."

"I can handle it," said the girl standing in front of him in the ragged sweater.

"And what does she look like?" he asked, just to make sure she had been listening.

"Her name is Athena. She's got blonde hair, shoulder length. Blue eyes ... and she'll be in the company of an olive-skinned woman named Fox. She looks Latino. And they'll both be at the Native American Conference in San Marcos." Irritated, she asked, "and you want me to do this why?"

"I need to get into her apartment and reclaim an oil picture that they stole from me."

"You sure you don't want to have sex with them?"

Crow shook his head no.

"I just need them out of the way for a time."

Noreen nodded okay and took the five, hundred-dollar bills he handed her.

"You can fly to Austin, rent a car, and make your way south to San Marcos. I'll cover your expenses. I'll cover any additional expenses you run up."

He found them at a reading table in the Georgetown Library on West Street quietly discussing racing forms. They were so intent that they did not see him enter, and so were surprised when he suddenly appeared looking down at them.

"You two the Basques," he asked … "from Idaho?"

They nodded and continued to stare.

He was strange looking to them … tall, taller even than they were, with black eyes, dark skin, and even, white teeth.

"I'm the one who placed the ad in the Boise paper, then talked to you on the phone … last week."

They did not respond, just kept staring at him.

He continued right on. "I'm Pico," he began, using the name of his former mentor rather than his own. "I have a job. Are you interested?"

He extended his hand to the one nearest to him.

The tallest one finally reached across the table and shook hands with him. Then Crow adjusted his black paper boy's hat which was sliding off.

"I'm Val Zu…."

"Please," interrupted Crow, "no last names. It's better that way. Who is this with you?"

Val turned towards the other Basque man, "This is my younger brother Adani, or Dani, as we like to call him."

Adani smiled up at Crow, then extended his hand and they shook.

"May I sit down to discuss," he hesitated a moment, "our business?"

They both nodded yes.

Crow noted the sausage fingers and strange nose – long and

aquiline like a bird's beak. Also, Dani's skin was beginning to show signs of rosacea.

They stared at each other momentarily.

Then, "Are you interested in my offer?" asked Crow.

"We don't kill nobody," said Dani matter-of-factly.

"If I wanted someone killed I would do it myself. That way I could be sure it was done properly ... without witnesses. And discreetly. Plus," he reassured them, "this is about stealing something."

"Good. We're interested," said Val. "What is it you want us to steal?"

"Two oil paintings. Not very valuable," he added. "I want you to steal them and destroy them."

Destroying the *Astride a Horse of Winter* would be just as effective as fixing the spell on it, he had decided finally.

"And how much will you pay?" asked Dani.

"Ten thousand."

"Each?" asked Dani.

Crow thought for a few seconds. "Sure. Ten thousand each."

"How will you pay us?" asked Val.

"Cash. No trail that way."

The two brothers discussed the offer in whispers.

Meanwhile, Crow opened a brown battered briefcase he had brought in with him and pointed to some cash, all in small bills.

"Half now, half when the job is done."

"How will we prove to you that we did it?" asked Val.

"Take a picture with your phone and send it to me."

They nodded acceptance.

"One more question," said Val. "How will we contact you?"

"You won't have to. I'll contact you."

"How?" asked Val.

"An ad in the obituaries of the Austin Statesman ... in the Memoriam section. It'll say, 'Remembering you with love, Monica.

Signed Mom and Dad'. Two days after this appears, I'll call you at the La Quinta in Round Rock, and arrange to the deliver the rest of the money."

Crow waited for a response.

"Any questions?"

"Yeah," said Val. "How will we know where the pictures are?"

"Good question. I almost forgot to tell you. I'll contact you tomorrow on your cell and let you know."

The brothers studied the money again.

"Do we have a deal?" asked Crow impatiently.

They nodded yes in unison.

⸺ ◦(◉)◦ ⸺

After Crow left, Val turned to Dani. "I don't think we should destroy the pictures, little brother. He's willing to pay us a lot of money to do it for him, but that just tells me that the pictures really are valuable."

Dani nodded. "So, what do you want to do with them?"

"Keep them, put them on the market, see what they'll fetch in California."

"But don't those kinds of pictures need a history?"

"Of course. We'll make one up."

"Okay," said Dani buying in with a big smile. "Sounds like a plan."

"We'll buy some cheap ones and burn them, then collect the remaining $10,000 from Mister Pico. "We'll show just enough of the pictures to convince him."

"He already thinks we're stupid, but we're not as dumb as he thinks. He underestimates us."

When Thena and Fox reached the lobby of the Comfort Inn a few days later Thena's cell phone rang. She checked the caller ID and discovered that it was Raven. Thena grabbed a seat in the lobby facing the fireplace.

"Hi," she said. "What's going on?"

"I made a fascinating discovery," replied Raven. "I have a book about spellcasting I thought you might be interested in."

"Oh?"

"Let me tell you first that I got this from a very old *Book of Shadows*. A member of my coven, Frannie Urban, bought it at a stall in a flea market in Hartville, Ohio. She is an antique nut and was on her way back from visiting her brother in Akron. She's had the book for several years now but never really looked into it. When we did, we discovered that the words for spells are not as important as the pitch pattern of the person's voice, his intonation, and stress. How well he says the words determines in large measure the effectiveness and power of the spell."

"Interesting," said Thena after a few moments of thinking about what Raven had told her. "But what about the icons, the Venus and the Helix?"

"Apparently, they're not even necessary for a very adept spell caster."

"So," said Thena, "some spell casters don't even need the icons. What they need to know is how to say, or sing, and chant the spell."

"Yes."

"Then how could Le Fey use your *Book of Shadows?*" asked Thena.

"Apparently, she couldn't … unless …."

"Unless what?" asked Thena.

"Unless she recorded me somehow and managed to mimic me perfectly."

"But no one could exactly reproduce your voice, and I trust you haven't recorded any spells."

"Yeah. I thought of that." She sighed. "Not that I remember."

"You'd better get the heck out of your house. I'm guessing that once she finds out that she needs you, she'll come back looking for you."

"Good advice," said Raven. "If you want me, call me on my cell."

"Okay," said Thena.

"Where are you headed next?"

"We're going to find Dreaming Woman and ask her to help us."

————))(((————

Fox waited patiently while Thena talked on the phone. When she rose, Fox pointed to a registration table where a heavily made up woman, tanned, and slightly over-weight sat making entries in a large, registration book. She was wearing a black and red Navajo patterned shirt.

When they reached the table, she looked up and smiled broadly. "Welcome to the thirty-fifth Texas Native American Conference. How can I help you?"

"We're looking for one of the Conference attendees ... a Susan Suisstanaka. Can you help us?"

The woman nodded yes, reached down, and pulled up a conference program. She opened to the Index of the book, scanned it briefly, and frowned. "She's not scheduled for anything at the moment, but may well be in the 'sweet grass' lobby."

She pointed to the entrance of the ballroom. When they entered, they saw sixty or more people, some in traditional native garb, sitting quietly at various tables. Many had their eyes closed and swayed to the drum beat being produced by a gray-haired gentleman who sang a ritual blessing in his native Navajo.

Fox saw Suisstanaka at a table in the northeast corner of the room and nudging Thena pointed to her. The medicine woman had her eyes closed and her arms crossed in front of her. Fox pointed again this time to a couple of empty chairs behind Suisstanaka's and they settled into them.

It was another half hour before the ceremony ended. Meanwhile Thena and Fox enjoyed the 'sweet grass' and felt themselves relaxing. The rhythmic chanting also helped to lull them.

They rose when Tanaka rose and walked slowly around to face her. When she saw them, she smiled.

"You're looking for me, aren't you?"

They both nodded yes.

"So," she began, after a brief pause, "what can I do for you?"

Thena took a moment and sized up the medicine woman. She was tall and thin with copper-colored skin, black eyes, and a straight, narrow nose. She also had long, flowing black hair. She looked like she could actually be native American, and yet there were subtle things about her appearance that made her look like no other person she had seen before.

Thena sighed deeply. "We came to ask for your help," she began. "Our lovers are trapped inside paintings and we want to free them before they are damaged by their captivity."

The medicine woman did not answer them immediately.

"Well?" asked Fox.

Dreaming Woman sighed.

"I have several questions?"

"Ask away," said Thena.

Fox also sighed deeply.

"I should tell you right up front … I don't know if I can release them from their bondage or not. Spells are tricky. It would be better if you could get the person who cast the spells to undo them."

Thena shrugged. "We would, but we don't know who cast them."

"How did you happen to come looking for me?"

"We know of you because of her sister." Thena pointed to Fox.

"Yeah," said Fox. "Morgan Le Fey."

"She was here yesterday, asking me to help her utilize two icons – a Helix sun sign, and a Venus moon sign. I tried to help her, but it did not go well."

"Why was that?" asked Thena.

"She struck me as suspicious. When I questioned her, she admitted that she had a book of spells but that she could not get any of them to work. She didn't seem to know that spellcasting depends on pitch and intonation."

"So, do you think you can help us?" asked Thena.

"I don't know. But I'll try if you bring me the pictures."

"What do you want in return?" asked Thena.

"Nothing. I don't need anything and I'm happy in my role, playing medicine woman."

The lobby of the motel was large with several events going on simultaneously.

The restaurant, El Poco, was off to the left of the lobby and at the front entrance was a series of event announcements mounted on large easels.

Ballroom One held 'The Native Peoples Conference,' where they had met Suisstanaka and Ballrooms Two and Three were hosting the traveling 'Best of the Day of The Dead' exhibit, which had recently been displayed at the Mexic-Arte Museum in Austin.

"I need to make a couple of calls to get the pictures here, but I'm going to completely trust you now," said Thena as she released the red cord controlling Fox.

"It'll take a few days to get the pictures here, even if I make contact with the person who has them right away. Do you have any interest in the 'Day of the Dead Exhibit' and are you hungry?"

"Yes, and yes," replied Fox with a big smile.

"Then, while I call, why don't you get us some tacos? Here's some money." She reached into her pocket and hauled out a fistful of change.

"Should I go to the café?"

"Why don't you ask the woman at the entrance of the Exhibit?"

Thena pointed to a woman at the entrance of Ballroom Two, dressed as a Catrina in an all-black, tight-fitting dress with a ghostly white, under-painted face and overpainted with ruby lips, black mascara around both eyes, and black pencil marks across both lips, representing stitch marks across upper and lower lips. Her eyes were large and her eyelash extensions were both long and black. Her hair was pulled back off her face and tied with a red scarf.

She looked like many of the women painted for 'Día de los Muertos,' beautiful underneath but with a reminder of mortality masked over it.

"There are food carts scattered among the exhibits," suggested the woman. "I'm sure one or two have tacos."

Fox pocketed the money and hurried into the exhibit.

The woman stood to the left of an arch, constructed of some wood Thena did not recognize.

"Pua wood," said the woman, when she saw Thena examining it. "It's sandalwood, finished with Iliahi powder mixed with coconut oil … quite fragrant."

"Seems out of place," she offered, "… like the motto above the door – 'Abandon Hope All Ye'."

"It's meant to be ironic, to lighten a traveler's journey through this Land of Death, like the 'Day of the Dead' celebrants themselves."

"I see," said Thena and handed her a five-dollar donation to support the continuation of the show.

She glanced into the entrance. It looked like a lighted tunnel, with subdued general lighting but with individual displays spotlighted. She could see sugar skulls, skeletons of all kinds, some painted on black velvet, some were sculpted tableaus of Death altars.

"What else is down there?" she asked the woman at the entrance.

"Well," she began, "a number of things. For example, Muertos dancers performing a story where at the end all the players fall down into coffins. There is an extensive collection of Zarco Guerrero fiberglass and hand carved wooden masks, including the famous white skull surrounded by blonde monkey hair. And," she continued, "between exhibits are carts offering different beers, tacos, and other things to eat, like skull-shaped suckers and ices from different, flavored skeleton part molds, and both packs and cartons of cigarettes of all brands."

<hr />

They reached the Zuckerman, large scale altar installation when Thena's cell phone rang. It was Marcus.

"Oh, look at the price!" said Fox. "Half of what the others ask." She was pointing at a Taco cart, manned by a young girl dressed as one of the 'Day of the Dead' dancers.

"You need more money?"

Fox nodded yes.

Thena handed her a ten-dollar bill. "Here. Get me two soft shelled beef tacos and a coke, please."

"Marcus," she began. "Glad you called. I was just about to call you."

"Oh? What'd you need?" he replied.

"I need the paintings … both of them. I'm in San Marcos. Fox and I have talked to a being named Suisstanaka who thinks she might know how to get both figures out of the paintings."

"Wonderful! It'll take me a couple of days to get them there. I'll drive them. It's safer that way."

"What do you mean safer, Marcus?"

"I was just thinking, if a picture were damaged how would it affect the man in it? Or, if someone painted over it. Would the men be the same or would they somehow be changed?"

"I don't know," she said. "I haven't really thought about it. Do you know?"

"No," he said. "I was just speculating about the consequences. They could be very bad."

Thena sighed.

"Sorry," he said. "I was just curious because I have the paintings in my custody."

Fox appeared with a cardboard carrier full of tacos and soft drinks.

"So, the sooner we get the men out of the paintings, the better?"

"Yes."

"Okay. How long do you think it will take you to get here?"

"Need to box them up properly and make the drive. I'm guessing two or three days at best."

"Call me when you hit the city limits, and I'll tell you exactly where to meet me."

<hr />

"Thanks for freeing me," said Fox.

Thena shrugged. "Keeping you prisoner is of no value to either me or Michael … oh, by the way what is the name of your friend in *The Disobedient?*"

"Wolfe, Ignatius Wolfe. I've missed him for a long time. At first, I didn't know what had happened to him. But I didn't want Morgan to know about him and I didn't know how to release him by myself. Turns out I was worried for nothing since she seems to know very little about spellcasting."

"I understand." Thena pressed Fox's hand quickly. "Look, it's clear to me that we need to get our men out of the paintings as soon as we can. They both appear to have powerful enemies."

Fox nodded.

"Until Marcus gets here, we've got a few days to kill. Let's go see what the 'Day of the Dead' art holds. It's supposed to be very original. For example, if you look at the women, you'll often see beauties painted over with Death … like the woman at the arch. Or the art will be ironic, a skeletal bride and groom. It represents the belief that death is a part of the wheel of life, and that old friends and ancestors are still with us."

"Do you think that is true?" asked Fox.

"Don't know, but look at you. If you had told me a year ago that someone like you could exist, I would have said you're out of your mind, and if you think a lot about someone who is dead, then that person does achieve a kind of immortality."

The women finished eating and headed for the arch leading to the gallery when everything began to melt and fuse. There were bright blasts of light and shards of paintings, like skeletal bones flying off randomly. Their world was spinning and they both passed out.

———— ◐ ————

Thena woke two days later in a bed at The Central Texas Medical

THE MICHAEL HOLLAND STORIES

Center with Fox in the bed next to her. She blinked several times to clear her vision and her mind. She was still slightly dizzy and could remember nothing except the spinning 'Day of the Dead' artifacts.

"Isn't this when I'm supposed to ask what happened?"

Fox just smiled at her and nodded.

From the sunlight streaming into the room it seemed like midafternoon. She reached down and pressed the assistance button, and saw the red light outside her door begin to blink.

Almost immediately, a smiling young man in a San Marcos police uniform stepped inside.

"A nurse is coming, Ma'am," he announced.

And almost before he finished, a nurse arrived and helped Fox out of bed.

"Good to see you awake, Thena," said Fox. "We ... I was worried about you."

A second nurse arrived, and they began to check the heart rate, and blood pressure of the two women.

"Is it okay if I talk to her?" asked the policeman.

The first nurse nodded yes. "Should be all right."

"Ma'am, my name is Jack Carter. I'm a San Marcos detective. From the lab results, we know that someone gave you a huge dose of ketamine, a date rape drug. It's normally a prescription drug. We know of the circumstances surrounding your dosing, and it doesn't appear that anyone was trying to rape you. Which brings up several questions. Do you feel like answering them?"

She nodded yes.

"Do you know of anyone who might want to hurt you ... or your friend?"

"No."

"Do you know of a man named Marcus Allensworth?"

"Yes, why do you ask?"

"He seems to be a part of this whole business."

Thena frowned, puzzled. "How so? And how do you know about him?"

"His van was hijacked last night just outside of Sonora. He told the Rangers who investigated that he was on his way to see you."

"Is he all right?" asked Thena.

"Seems to be," Carter replied, "but the vehicle is gone, along with its contents. He said that there were two paintings in it that he was bringing to you. He feels bad about the loss, so much so that he has been mildly sedated and put in the hospital in Sonora."

"What hospital?"

"The Lillian Hudspeth, just off I-10."

"Can I call him?" asked Thena.

"I suppose," the officer paused and added, "so, to summarize, he was on his way to meet you with art in his van?"

She nodded yes.

"Is the art valuable?"

"Yes, but not in the millions of dollars range."

"Can you describe the pictures for us?"

She did in detail, leaving out the part that each had a real person in it. Carter took copious notes. Then he excused himself to go and send this information to various law enforcement agencies throughout the state.

"What are we going to do now?" asked Fox who had been quietly listening to the conversation.

"We need to work fast. I don't know this for certain, but if the pictures are damaged it may affect Michael and Wolfe. Marcus was concerned about that possibility."

"So, what do we do?"

"We set a thief to catch a thief."

"What do you mean?"

"Do you see my wallet there in the Coach bag?"

Fox nodded yes.

"Dig it out and hand it to me."

She did as Thena had requested and then watched as she dug into the wallet and found a folded up, small piece of paper behind her driver's license. The flap had been tucked in, but Fox could see that across the back flap was an outlined flower, a marigold in black.

Thena saw Fox looking at the slip curiously. "Yes. It is a black marigold, the sign of a former lover of Michael's. And as much as I hate doing this, I'm going to anyway. She is, I've been told, one of the world's great art thieves. And we seem to need a great thief if we are to get the pictures back quickly."

———◦(◦)◦———

Thena saw her coming down the ramp from the plane and she knew her immediately. She felt her heart sink. Lilly was truly beautiful – long black hair down to her shoulder blades, slim, radiant green eyes, and a perfect, if small, figure.

She could understand why Michael couldn't resist her, and she immediately felt a flash of jealousy. How could she compete with a beautiful and successful Romani?

Yet, she needed her. She could not get Michael out of the painting if she didn't have the painting. Lilly was the best thief she knew of … and perhaps the only one who could get the pictures back quickly. The others, she only knew through her police work. So, she swallowed hard and determined to befriend the Romani.

Lilly was all in black … form fitting black jeans, black leather boots, and a black, sleeveless, but simple, top.

Thena sighed deeply and waited for Lilly at the foot of the baggage ramp. She smiled broadly, even though she felt inadequate.

Lilly saw her almost at the same time and when she reached the bottom of the escalator, walked over to her.

"Ah, my little blonde girl!"

"What?"

She immediately saw that Thena was upset and launched into an explanation. "It was meant as a symbol of affection."

"Good," replied Thena, "because I'm as tall as you are."

"So, you are. Stand there a second. Let me take a look at you."

Lilly looked her up and down, and then clicking her tongue softly as she moved, slowly circled her.

"Michael is a lucky man. You are truly as beautiful as he said you were."

"Thank you," said Thena, suddenly ashamed and embarrassed.

"Had I seen you in Paris -- I understand you spent a semester there -- I would have tried to bed you."

Thena flushed.

Lilly shrugged and then sensing Thena's discomfort, explained, "I can't help myself. I'm attracted to beauty, and you certainly are beautiful."

"Thank you again."

Just then the bags began to appear on the conveyor belt.

"That's mine," she exclaimed and leaped in front of Thena to grab one.

Thena watched as Lilly wrestled the bag off the belt, and in spite of her misgivings found that she liked the Romani -- a lot.

And if she had tried to bed her, Thena might have let her. She toyed with the idea and smiled a great deal.

On the way to the car, Lilly asked Thena how she had gotten her phone number.

"In one of the notes you left for Michael. I found it in his wallet."

"Really! He was supposed to destroy my notes," she replied.

"Look," began Thena, "I'm not necessarily thrilled to have you here, but thank God he didn't. Otherwise, I wouldn't have had any idea how to find you."

Lilly nodded that she understood.

"I have a car in the parking deck. Do you have other luggage?"

"Only this one and my carry-on."

Thena led the way. Shortly, they reached the car.

"I'm surprised you came," said Thena, as she maneuvered out of the airport and headed for San Marcos.

"So am I," replied Lilly. "But your story was too intriguing to ignore. I needed to find out for myself. And, by the way, I really do care for Michael."

"I know," admitted Thena, "but my story is true. There are beings from other worlds here, some for thousands of years, who can do things I never imagined, and who have probably precipitated mythologies around the world. As far as I know they have never been to their own world of origin."

"It's hard to believe."

"I know. If I hadn't seen Michael absorbed into a painting with my own eyes, I would have been as dubious as I'm sure you are."

"And what happened to the paintings," asked Lilly.

"The van was hijacked two nights ago, near Sonora, about 200 miles west of here."

"And, I understand, the Texas Rangers are working on the robbery? Is that correct?"

Thena nodded yes, then added, "But I need to get the pictures back as soon as I can. While we know that if left alone, it takes a long time for the real people trapped in the pictures to come to harm, we don't know what happens to those individuals if a picture itself is damaged or painted over."

"So, you called me?"

"According to Michael, you're the best. And frankly I didn't know how to find an art thief in a short amount of time. Most art criminals I've had any contact with either don't appreciate what they have or they got the art in some 'grab and run' scheme … mostly from private homes or from some poorly guarded museum collection."

"True. Most of the owners are not too careful. So, where are we going now?" asked Lilly when she noticed that Thena wasn't headed for downtown Austin.

"A hospital in Sonora to see the man who was robbed, a friend of Michael's … and my guardian. He'll get this recovery process started. By the way, you don't look anything like I imagined a *gitano* would. You are quite sexy."

"Thanks. There are gypsies and there are gypsies. Most are highly secretive and committed to maintaining the old ways. But more and more, they are giving up their independence and fun-loving and becoming idle, homeless burdens on the governments of any country who recognizes them. Besides I'm only half *gitano*. My mother was an extremely bright, independent woman who taught art at the Sorbonne. And as I figure you already know there is a Christian myth that says that Jesus granted gypsies the right to steal because of their efforts to save him from the cross …."

"Ah, the lost nails myth."

"Yes. And my side of the family decided that if we were going to steal, it would be with impunity and worth the effort."

"So, you and yours are the well-off gypsies, then?"

"We are. And we are good at what we do. We've studied the art of theft and tried to master it."

"By the way, I am glad you could get here so quickly."

Lilly shrugged. "I was in L.A. planning a job when my message service called with your request."

"And you still came?"

"Of course. You piqued my curiosity. And, the art will still be there. In fact, no outsiders are even supposed to know the art exists."

"Oh!"

"It belongs to a very wealthy man, a film director, who has a secret, underground gallery beneath his mansion where he collects illegal art that only a few intimates get to see. I was waiting for his security codes through a bribe of his chauffeur."

"But even if you stole several pieces, how would you make money from them? Wouldn't the police track you down?"

"You forget, the art is illegal. Its owner isn't going to put out a police alarm about it being stolen. If he did, then he would have to explain how he got it in the first place. It would alert the real owners that he had it, and potential thieves like me that might want to steal it. It would likely cause him more problems than he could imagine … not to mention what it might do to his reputation."

"So, what would you do with it if you successfully stole it?"

She smiled. "That's easy. I would ransom it back to the owner at much less than the piece is worth, but still large enough to guarantee me a nice profit. I'm very good at what I do."

"I believe it. But it takes a certain kind of chutzpah to do what you do."

"I'm a gypsy," she explained.

"You don't look like a gypsy. In fact, you don't look like I expected you would."

"Oh? Well," Lilly smiled, "in all honesty I wear green contacts sometimes to change my look. My eyes are naturally very dark but surely, you're not stereotyping me on the basis of how gypsies are portrayed in film, are you?"

"No, no. I didn't mean anything other than you are quite beautiful, more beautiful than I remember when I saw you in Paris."

"Oh, you saw me in Paris?"

"Yeah. But it was at a distance. And, of course, Michael described you to me."

"What did he tell you?"

"Only that you were a superb thief and that he met you at Columbia, was dazzled by your looks, and left school to follow you to Europe. He also said that he got involved in some sort of trouble and basically disconnected himself from you and your companions in some burst of moral indignation. Which, I believe he later came to regret."

"That's a fairly accurate short version. Did he tell you that he was the one, not my cousins who dubbed me Black Marigold?"

"No. He left that part out."

"Yeah, after that damned romantic poem that he gave me to express his feelings. Up till then I didn't realize how terribly naïve he was."

"And still is. But he has his code."

"I know," she explained. "We were, and still are, very different people. You are much more compatible with him than I am. I knew after a few months that he and I could never be a couple. I am what I am. And I cannot change."

"Does that mean you'll give up bedding him?"

Lilly smiled. "Can't. It's what I do. I change people I sleep with. It's my nature. As you have already figured out, I don't believe in monogamy. It's unnatural."

"I guess I'm eventually going to have to tell him that I took your note out of his wallet."

Lilly chuckled. "Of course, but if we get him out of the art, he'll be so grateful he won't care. And if he's still concerned, remember you're named after Athena, the goddess of wisdom who oversaw Odysseus' journey home. I'm confident you'll think of something."

<hr />

It was mid-afternoon when they arrived at the Hudspeth Hospital in Sonora. Marcus was looking tired and old. But he was out of his bed and sitting by a window streaming with sunlight.

He tried to rise when he saw the two women at the door to his room, but Thena hurried over and pushed him back down into his chair. "Rest," she said.

"I'm so sorry …"

"It's all right. We'll get the art back. In fact, the woman with me is Lilith, better known as Lilly, a friend of Michael's. She's going to help me get the pictures back."

"I know who you are … a very capable art thief."

Lilly smiled. "And how do you know of me?" she asked.

"You're the Black Marigold. Michael told me all about you," he admitted.

"I'm flattered."

"We're going to set a thief to catch a thief. And since time is critical, I got the very best person I knew of, and I've brought her to you."

He watched Thena carefully. "I'm surprised. I didn't think …"

"… that I would ask her?" finished Thena.

"Something like that."

"Well, I did. So, you need to tell her all you can remember."

And he did.

⋙ ⋘

"Start when they, whoever they are, took your van with the pictures in it," said Lilly.

He nodded that he understood. "The police eventually recovered the van, somewhere close to Austin. Obviously, they just took the vehicle … maybe they didn't even realize that here were two pictures in it. I mean – how would they know?"

"Don't kid yourself. They knew exactly where you were. And what was in the van."

"But, how could they?" Marcus asked.

Lilly shrugged. "I don't know yet, but there are ways. What we can assume is that someone wanted one, or both, of the paintings. Perhaps, they overheard one of you talking about the paintings and assumed they were valuable. Or," she continued, "someone put a tracking device on your van, and they followed you for a way waiting for the right opportunity. Or, maybe they had a bug on your phone."

"Couldn't be. I've been using burner phones, especially since all that has happened to me recently. No evidence, but very suspicious."

"Aha! So, tell me what has been happening to you lately."

Marcus proceeded to tell her of the suspicious events that had befallen him in the past few months, including what had happened to Sylvia. He even included his taking of a medical leave from the university.

"Where did you come from?" asked Lilly, after she had digested what he had told her.

"I came from the Days Inn in Lubbock that morning. Down Route 87 to I-10. I had the paintings stashed there, so I flew in and rented a van to transport them to Austin."

"Do you remember anything about them?"

"I never actually saw whoever stole the van, but there were two suspicious men ... I saw them first in the Denver airport. Now that you mention it, they also showed up at the Days Inn."

"Remember anything about them?"

He nodded, "Both taller than me, about six feet or so, both unshaven and stocky, and one of them, the one I assumed to be the dominant one, spoke to the other in a language I did not recognize. He called the other one Eskualdun and mentioned 'boys.'"

Lilly's face lit up. "I know who they are," she said, as a matter-of-fact. "Not specifically, but I recognize the language. They are from a Basque colony in Boise, Idaho. Not too many Basques there, but that's good. Fewer means we can figure out who they are. Makes it easier to find them. Did you tell the State Patrol what you just told me?"

He nodded yes.

"Then we need to get out of here right now," said Thena. "Because if they find the art before we do, it'll become evidence. And we'll have a hell of a time getting the men out of the art."

"She's right," said Lilly.

Thena reached into her purse, pulled out a phone, handed it to Marcus.

"If you think of anything else, call me on this. It's prepaid."

He nodded and they left.

"Will you drive?" asked Lilly.

When they were on the road again, Thena said, "I'm impressed. How did you make that connection so quickly?"

"Partly luck. As you already know, I'm part French and part Romani. And once when I was very young and visiting Saintes-de-los-Maries for the annual festival a young man from Lower Navarre rode into the sea with the rest of us. When I was just about up to my chin, a huge wave knocked me off my stallion. The young man, Koldo Orbea saw me flailing among my horse's legs and pulled me up behind him on his own stallion. I don't think I would have drowned, I was a very good swimmer, even then. But later that night around a huge bonfire on the beach, I found out what his real talent was."

"And what was that?"

"He could sing, play guitar, and compose original songs, virtually on the spot. He was a 'bertsolari' troubadour, as the others called him. One of his songs, in particular, was haunting, *Black Rock*, about peacefulness found in the mountains. I never forgot him, though we eventually went our separate ways. I became a thief and he, a vocal proponent of Basque nationalism."

"What happened to him eventually," asked Thena, quite absorbed in the story.

"Someone assassinated him a few years ago while he was drinking coffee at a left bank café with a woman he was planning to marry."

"Did they ever find out who did it?"

"The authorities arrested a young, disabled man, as I recall. He had some mental, or personality issue. They held him for a longtime, but they never got any useful information out of him. There were some eyewitnesses, but they could not identify him, and they eventually let him go. He was, of course, a gypsy, and Parisians do not like gypsies. They think they are just freeloaders."

"I'm sorry," said Thena.

"So am I. Koldo was a good guy."

After a brief silence Lilly asked, "Where are we headed?"

"We're headed up state route 87 to see if we can find Marcus's rest stop," answered Thena.

"I'm going to make a phone call and pretend to be someone else. Try not to laugh when you hear me."

Thena nodded okay and watched as Lilly punched in Directory Assistance.

"I need the phone number for the Boise, Idaho, city police."

A few seconds passed and then, "Yeah. Connect me with that number, please."

It was late November and darkness gathered fast.

Then, "Is this Desk Sergeant Bobbie Davis? Hello, Sergeant Davis, this is Connie Wilde of the Texas State Highway Patrol. Yeah, badge number 2324. I've been looking into an art theft. Occurred two days ago. Based on evidence from the victim, I have reason to believe the thieves have some connection to Boise."

"Yes, I understand that it is snowing heavily there and all available officers are out of the office. But these two thieves spoke a strange language and one called the other Eskualdun. Does that mean anything to you?"

"Basque, you say. I'll be damned. Can you take down this description?"

She gave him the description Marcus had given her, and her cell phone number.

"A detective Marino will call me back as soon as he is able. Got it. Thanks, and be careful on those slippery roads."

And Lilly hung up.

Thena smiled broadly at her. "My God!" she began. "What a con job. I'm in awe."

Lilly smiled back at her, and Thena felt her heart skip a beat.

"It all has to do with confidence, some small amount of acting ability, and bravado."

"Is there really a Connie Wilde, highway patrol woman?"

"As a matter of fact, there is. I've even got her badge number in case he checks. But my guess is that no one will. After all it's snowing heavily there. They will have more important things to do. The sergeant will probably just pass the message along to Detective Marino and forget about it."

———※《◎》※———

It was well after dark before Thena found the spot where Marcus's van had been stolen. It was a southeast bound rest area about twenty minutes from Sonora. They parked and got flashlights from the glovebox. Thena also took a small caliber pistol from her purse that Michael had given her for protection … and began to walk the premises.

Fifteen minutes into the search, Lilly called for Thena to join her next to the vending area. When she caught up with her, Lilly was holding a cigarette box, mostly sky blue with the words 'Tor Turkish' on the front above the very specific warning that 'Smoking can harm you.'"

"What does it mean?" asked Thena.

"The Basques are very fond of Turkish and Russian cigarettes. Blue papered Tor and black papered Sobranie's are their favorites. This confirms my suspicions about the crooks. When, and if, Detective Marino calls, maybe I'll mention it to him."

She nodded.

"Meanwhile, I'm going to gather information on the van."

"How are you going to do that?"

Lilly snickered. "Oh, little dear one. You have so much to learn. So, who would have the van information … besides Marcus?" She answered her own question. "The police. So, I'm going to call the Sonora police department. They'll know." She snickered again, and then made the call.

When she was done, desk sergeant Bill Donovan had identified the black and green van rental service for her, the Marvel Auto Rental, and she and Thena were on their way to Austin. A second call from Detective Marino identified the two thieves as Val and Adani Zulaika. He explained that while there were a number of Basques in Boise, very few were criminals. So, he knew the Turkish smoking brothers easily. Though, he said he had not seen them for about month. When he asked their mother about them, she told him that they had gotten jobs in Austin, Texas. She said that it had come to them over the internet.

They left early so they could stop at a few casinos on the way … seems they like how they are treated there.

"Thank you, Detective Marino. That will help us find them."

"May I ask why you are looking for them?"

"They stole two paintings from a van at a rest stop just northwest of Sonora."

"Curious," he replied. "That's not their kind of crime. They wouldn't know what to do with the art unless someone told them to ransom the pictures. You might look at the East Coast or California markets. I'm guessing that their job was to steal them and then turn them over to someone else … probably the person who hired them. They're more likely to stickup a convenience store for some small change so they can gamble online or in one of those store front operations."

"Thanks," said Lilly. "If you get a line on where they might be, would you mind letting me know?"

"Glad to."

Lilly hung up.

"You didn't mention the Turkish cigarettes," said Thena.

"I know, but I didn't want some gung-ho policeman getting to the art before we did. They would impound it and lock it up,"

"So, what's our next move?" asked Thena as they drove towards Austin.

"We need to find them."

"How?"

"Let your fingers do the walking … a line from an old ad."

And she was on her phone again.

"Directory assistance? I need the number of a Mrs. Zulaika in Boise, Idaho. Yes, I'll hold. Please connect me." She turned to Thena. "Remember this, in case we have to call her again. 208-908-7434, South Vista Avenue."

A few moments passed. Then, "Hello. Mrs. Zulaika, I'm a friend of your son Val ... met him last night at the Rodeo South Bar on 6th street in Austin. He offered me the most wonderful Turkish cigarette. He told me how to order them online ... Tor Turkish, I believe ... But I've lost the website and I don't know how to reach him here. My name is Olivia Smith."

A few more moments pass. "You don't either. Oh! Certainly. I'll hold." A few more moments pass.

"Okay, Bonds in London. Bonds, you say. Thank you. I'm sure if I google them, I can get their website, Sorry to bother you. Thanks again."

"You are remarkable," said Thena.

"Experience," she replied. "It's only 5 o'clock there. Let's call them."

Again, Lilly got the number from directory assistance and dialed.

"Hi," she began. "Glad you're still open. I'm Samantha Jones, Texas State Trooper, calling on my cell from just outside Austin. I'm trying to locate two fugitives involved in the hijacking of a van, and in tracking them, I discovered from their mother that one of them, a Val Zulaika, just ordered four cartons of Tor Turkish cigarettes from you. I was wondering if you would tell me where you're sending them? I'd really appreciate your cooperation in this matter."

Another long pause.

"Aha. I understand that you have a privacy policy, and I respect that. So, I'll have someone from Scotland Yard stop by as soon as you open in the morning with proper paper work."

She got half way through 'Thank you' when she suddenly stopped.

"The Wyndham Garden Hotel, 3401 South I-35. Thank You. I really appreciate it." And then she punched out the number. "Thank goodness they didn't want Scotland Yard showing up," she laughed.

"You're amazing!" said Thena with a big smile.

"As I said before, experience, a little bit of acting, and a lot of confidence are not to be undervalued."

"Still, you are amazing."

She shook her head no. "I'm a thief, stealing from some very bright, if corrupt people. I've taught myself to think one step … sometimes two or three ahead of them … like a chess game. I have to anticipate their every move. And, honestly, sometimes they outfox me."

"I see," said Thena, "Still … you do have skills. Where to now?"

"The Wyndham, south Austin … by the way do you still have that gun handy?"

"I do. But remember it's only a .22 caliber pistol."

"Doesn't matter. I don't intend to shoot them. I just want to scare them."

"Damn, damn, damn," said Crow. "You almost killed them!"

Noreen glanced down at her feet. Then looked up with a smile and a shrug.

"How much did you give them?"

"Sorry," said Noreen. "I figured if a dose would knock them out, I'd double it – just to make sure."

They were walking by the river in Zilker Park, in South Austin. Crow stared out at the water.

"Okay, okay. I guess I shouldn't punish you for being overexuberant. You did good." He reached into his pocket and pulled out a wad of bills. "How much did you spend?" he asked.

She reached into her own pocket and pulled out a sheet of paper. "It's all there."

And she handed the itemized sheet to him.

He studied it for a few seconds and then handed her several bills. "Are you available if I need someone to help me in the future?"

She nodded yes.

"Okay. Go back to Ft. Collins. Do you have a cell phone?"

She shook her head no.

"Get one and call me at this number to tell me what your phone number is."

She smiled broadly and accepted more money.

———◦《◊》◦———

It was a little after 8 pm when the door of room 211 in the Wyndham Hotel swung open and two hulking, unshaven men entered.

The women were sitting in half light, cast by the bathroom.

"I guess I should have checked to see if the track was still open," said the taller of the two.

"Yeah," said the other, "but that poker game we ran into was very cool. And I made almost 500 bucks!"

"Who's that?" asked Val, gesturing towards a woman near the bathroom.

"Where?" asked Dani. Then, noticing the woman all in black straddling the chair near the bathroom door, "Did you call for a hooker, Val. And what's it gonna' cost us?"

Val shook his head no. "I didn't Dani. And, I don't know where she came from."

With a smile, Lilly said, "Sorry, boys. I'm not a hooker, and we did not come here to entertain you in any way, much less sexually. I hate to disappoint you, but you're not our type."

"Then why are you here?" asked Val.

Thena had been watching from the end of the couch at the foot of the double bed. Her gun was drawn and leveled at them.

"Wow!" said Dani softly, "Another beauty. Too bad you ladies don't want to party. My brother and I can show you a good time. He brought back a bottle of twenty- year old Dewar's scotch we won in a poker game."

"We came for the art?" said Thena.

"We thought Mr. Pico was going to pick it up. After we sent him the pictures of us burning the art, we put them into storage."

"So, you burned the pictures!" exclaimed Thena, shocked.

"No, no, no," said Val. "We figured they were worth some dough, since he was paying us $10,000 each to steal them. So, we burned two we bought cheap, and put the ones we stole from the van into a storage facility. We figured we'd see what kind of price the paintings would fetch. Somewhere far away so he wouldn't catch on."

"So, you were going to cheat Mr. Pico. When he caught you, you then admitted what you were going to do and told him you put them into storage."

Both men nodded sheepishly.

"We didn't tell him what we were going to do since we didn't do it. But he caught on. So, we told him the pictures were in storage."

"So, are they?" asked Lilly. "I'm getting confused. Where are the pictures now?"

"In the South Austin Storage Unit down the road from here."

"We need to see them to make sure they aren't damaged."

"By the way, how did you know we were the ones who stole them."

Lilly smiled. "Blue papered Turkish cigarettes. At the rest stop. One of you dropped a pack."

"So," said Val, "Not only good looking but smart too."

"Okay," said Lilly. "Enough chitchat. You come with us now and show us where you stored the art. Then, you can get it out of the unit and we'll go from there."

"No way," began Dani. "We're not giving you the art unless we get the rest of the money Mr. Pico owes us."

"He'll get it to you," said Thena, playing on their belief that Mr. Pico sent them to pick up the pictures.

"Nope," said Dani, digging in his heels. "No money, no art."

The women looked chagrined.

"Besides it's raining out and I don't fancy getting wet again. I need a drink. Open the Dewar's, Val."

"See my blonde friend over there," Lilly nodded towards Thena. "That thing in her hand is a pistol and it's aimed at you. Don't be fooled by her good looks, she knows how to use it."

Thena raised the pistol again and aimed it at Dani.

"Now hold on," began Val. "No need to get nervous. We can take you there and explain to whoever is on the gate that you can get into the unit any time you want to."

"Come on," said Lilly, "both of you."

"Okay, okay. Whatever you want. But I thought that Spanish guy, Pico, was going to pick up the art tomorrow morning and pay us."

"Give me your checking account number and the name of your bank, and I'll transfer the money he owes you when our bank opens in the morning,"

"Christ, Lady! Do we look like we have a checking account?"

She looked them over, then reconsidered. "You've got a point. I'll tell you what … find me an ATM and I'll give you all I can take out, probably $500. When Chase opens in the morning, I'll get a cashier's check for the rest of it. How much is it by the way?"

"Ninety-five hundred more, if you give us $500 now."

"Hold on, hold on. I think they need to give us what we have coming before we show them the pictures," said Dani.

"Okay," agreed Lilly. "We don't have to get the pictures now. But we need to see them, to be sure they're not damaged."

"Do we look like we would damage something as valuable as the art?"

"Not if you thought you were going to get paid for it. But things happen. So, let's go."

"Alright," said Val. "We'll lead, you follow."

Lilly nodded okay.

"It's the black van in the parking lot with the splash of bright green across the hood," said Val.

<hr />

When they got to the South Austin Storage facility, Thena breathed a sigh of relief because the building advertised on its face that it was climate controlled. And, she wasn't sure that the paint wouldn't just run. She nudged Lilly and looked up at the statement.

Lilly nodded, and they followed the Zuliaka brothers into the storage complex.

The man at the gate, an older, paunchy, man in his 60's, nodded at them as they passed through.

They parked both vehicles in front of building 4 and entered.

"Unit 171 is on the first floor. We go down the hall to the right and when it ends, we go right again."

The unit was large, sat on a concrete floor, and had a corrugated metal door. Thena stood behind Val with her hand on the pistol as he thumbed open the combination lock and pulled up the door.

The two paintings, looking lonesome, sat in their wooden crates on opposite walls and were covered with large tarps. "We'll just check out the paintings to make sure they are the correct ones," said Lilly.

Then she turned to Thena, "Keep your pistol on them, and if they do anything funny, be sure to shoot each one in the knee. It's painful, but won't kill them."

"I'm just going to check to make sure these are the right pictures." The brothers nodded all right, and while Thena kept her pistol trained on them, Lilly unpacked the pictures. When they had confirmed that they were the proper paintings, Lilly put them back into their crates.

"Satisfied?" asked Val.

The women nodded yes.

"Okay," stated Lilly. "Here's the deal. We'll meet you here at 10:30 tomorrow morning after the bank opens and we get the rest of the money for you. Agreed?"

The men nodded once more.

Val pulled down the door and locked it. Then, he started down the hallway.

Dani walked beside him. Lilly and Thena walked a few steps behind them.

"I saw you taking a video of the combination with your phone," whispered Lilly. "You sly dog."

Thena smiled.

"So, we get a room close by and come back later?"

"Three or four hours, ought to be enough," said Lilly.

<hr />

They took a room at the Hampton and waited, each with a margarita.

"I understand that you were the one who broke off the relationship with Michael. True?" asked Thena.

"Not really. He just up and left one day."

"Didn't you love him anymore?"

"I still do. The parting was painful. But he gave me that *Black Marigolds* poem. He got it from Steinbeck's *Cannery Row* and I was flattered. Then, he started calling me Vidya, after the woman in the poem and his black marigold because of my black hair and eyes.

And I suddenly knew how naïve he was. And that the relationship wouldn't last. He tells everyone who asks that my cousins dubbed me Black Marigold because he's embarrassed to admit that he was the one who did it."

"Yeah, he can be like that sometimes."

"It all got to be too corny after a while. I wanted him, I ached for him, but I always knew who I was … and still am. We were in different worlds, not just physically but psychologically as well. And if he had stayed with me, I would have corrupted him. I didn't want to be responsible for that. He would have eventually come to hate me. I am what I am. And I know I'm not going to change. In fact, I don't want to change. I like what I am. I just want to get better at it."

Thena sipped her drink. "Don't you realize that sooner or later, you'll get caught?"

"Maybe, maybe not. That's part of the thrill. I know of a few other thieves at my level. Many are even known to the authorities, but knowing who we are and proving it are two entirely different issues. In the art world, even successful thieves are not always too bright. Their greed tends to trip them up. You can find a couple of good examples in the art-theft book, *Priceless*."

"Do you regret him going away?"

"Yes," admitted Lilly. "Especially that Jason beard he grew after we saw Steve Reeves in *The Argonauts* movie. It was so cute and he was so happy with himself. But it dawned on me, especially after we went to Saintes Maries for the Black Madonna festival that he was much less mature than me. After all, I was raised in close contact with my Dad's *gitan family* – all of whom were accomplished thieves and believed that they had a right to steal because of that Jesus story."

"It's not out of the ordinary," remarked Thena. "There is a tribe in the Trobriand Islands where stealing is not only encouraged but how it was done is honored. The creativity of it is important."

"I've heard of them," said Lilly. "But we're not in those islands."

"I know," said Thena, as she stared at Lilly and suddenly felt deep affection for her. "Let's go get those pictures," she said changing the subject.

As they drove to the storage unit, Thena remarked, "okay, say we get the pictures, what do we do with them until I can get Dreaming Woman to release the human figures in them?"

"Hide them in plain sight," said Lilly "not literally, but we'll rent a unit in the same storage facility until you can catch up with Dreaming Woman, and we'll bring them to her."

"Brilliant! I was hoping you had some plan for them."

"And what about the $9,500 we promised the Zulaikas?"

"I'll pay them. It'll get them out of our hair … kind of buy us a bit of insurance."

"That's a lot of money."

"Yeah. But aren't you curious about who they are really working for?"

"Yes, somehow I don't think it's Pico."

"Agreed, he seems too cool to try to steal the pictures. Michael and I saw him in Montreal. There's more going on here than we know, and frankly, I don't like being in the dark."

"Well, I don't want them hounding us. And in the long run they might prove useful."

"How so?" asked Thena.

"Don't know yet. Muscle … transportation. And they have had some contact with whoever ordered the theft, whether it is Pico or not, and we might be able to find out why someone else is interested in the pictures."

"But our first priority has got to be to get the men out of the pictures."

"Agreed."

A few minutes later they stood looking at unit 171. Thena dialed the combination, and they lifted the door together. They looked into the darkness, lit only by the light from the hall way. Lilly turned on her flashlight, and they stood stunned – the room was empty.

———— ———— ————

They drove back to their motel in silence, each trying to think of logical reason for the disappearance of the pictures.

Still without speaking, they pulled into a convenient parking spot, locked the car, and headed into the Irish Pub connected to the restaurant in the motel.

Lilly sighed.

Thena turned to her and asked "Tanqueray and tonic, okay?"

Lilly nodded yes.

Thena ordered two.

When they arrived, Lilly said, "Bring me two too," she snickered, when the barkeep cocked his head to ask if she was serious. "Just kidding. But I'll probably need another one later."

"You don't seriously think that Val and Dani were smart enough to go back and move them before we got there?"

"That's exactly what I think," said Lilly. "The two dolts outsmarted us. Maybe there is just enough smarts between them to think of doing exactly what we were going to do."

"We can check with the attendant on duty," offered Thena.

"And we should. Then we should go back to their room and confront them. If they aren't smart enough to pull this off on their own, then someone who is very bright is at least one step ahead of me … and that really makes me mad. Ego, ego, ego! I was so damned cock sure. An amateur mistake."

"Let's approach this logically," said Thena. "It's only been a little more than three hours since we were at Unit 171 with the boys. Let's list the possibilities. First, they were just sly enough to have moved them. They couldn't have known that the pictures had real people in them, so they must have had another purpose for the art."

"They were going to collect from Pico and sell the real pictures on the black market, probably in California, far enough away from here so that whoever asked them to steal them would not recognize them."

"They would have had to had that idea before we even found them, which means they rented a second unit right off the bat."

"And that means the pictures are still somewhere in the storage facility," added Lilly.

"Or," continued Thena, "this Pico could have come and picked them up. He would have had to have an SUV to put them in."

"Again, we could ask the attendant if an SUV entered in the last few hours."

"Or, third, someone else was tracking them from the beginning of Marcus' trip. It wouldn't be Fox. She wants the picture called *The Disobedient* as badly as I want *Astride a Horse of Winter*. It might be Le Fey, but I don't know why she would want them. In and of themselves, they're not that special, and if it was some other party, they he would have to have a ready-made market."

"That means that whoever he was, if it was a third party, would have to know what we know."

"So, what do you want to do next?" asked Lilly as she sipped her drink.

"Back to the office of the storage complex, where we are going to find out who's renting a second unit."

"Hack their computer?" asked Lilly.

"Absolutely." Then, Thena suddenly looked over at Lilly, a quizzical smile on her face. "You can, right."

"Of course. That's how I get a lot of my information."

Thena had used her phone camera to record all the combinations Val used, so getting into the storage unit was no problem, nor was getting into the office.

Once there, Lilly fired up the Acer, broke the code and was into the facility's files in very short order. It took only a few moments to copy the files to a thumb drive in case they had to access them again. A few short moments later Lilly announced that the Zulakais had no other unit listed in either of their names, 25% were empty, and there was no one listed with the first name of Pico.

Lilly frowned.

"What are you thinking?" asked Thena.

"That the art is still in this facility. If I were them, I wouldn't rent a second unit in my own name either. So, I'm thinking about aliases."

"Like?"

"Maybe their mother's first name or maiden name."

"Any suspicious names?"

"Here's one ... Devil's Ride."

"What an odd name for the patron of a storage unit."

"It's the name of a game, like poker," explained Lilly. "Let's check it out ... see what's in the unit."

Thena nodded all right.

They exited the office and found the unit rented under the name Devil's Ride. Lilly opened it in a few minutes. When the door was pushed up, all was dark. She turned on the flashlight they had brought for the occasion, and there in the back of the unit was a card table with a black trash bag on it.

They flicked on the overhead. Lilly nodded to Thena, "you do the honors, this time."

She nodded okay and approached the bag. It was tied at the top, and she carefully undid the knot there, reached inside, and pulled out a large book, about one foot high by a foot and a half across. It was bound in red leather, and across the cover were the words in gold letters two inches high, *Book of the Horned God.*

They stood in awe for several long moments. Then Thena spoke, "What can we do with this?"

"Nothing, my dear … nothing. Bag it back up and let's get out of here – fast!" she cautioned.

"Shouldn't we … "

"If this is what I think it is, and it's the real thing, then we need to get out of here as quickly as we can. If it is, then we've stumbled into something we don't want to be involved with under any circumstance."

———————

Once they were safely back in their car and out of the facility, Thena asked Lilly about the book.

"Okay, Lilly, what is it about that book that scares you?"

"It's Lucifer's book, his *Book of Shadows,* of spells, if you will."

"But he's gone," protested Thena. "Michael and I disposed of him."

"So, I heard, but when he comes back, if he does, he'll be looking for revenge."

"Maybe, but I'll be ready for him," said Thena "and if I have Michael back, he'll have to face both of us again."

"Well I hope you're right, but you don't know him like I do, and I think you're underestimating him. I think you two got lucky the first time. He underestimated you … and you caught him by surprise."

"You don't understand" she corrected, "we had a plan, we were counting on his immense ego to work in our favor. And it did."

"But you can't trick him again. He's a quick learner, and he'll be ready for the two of you. And when we get Michael out of that art, I'll tell him the same thing. So, think about what you're going to do when he returns. You need an even better plan. He's one smart cookie, and he's ruthless."

"I will," said Thena, chagrined.

They each took a moment to think about the book.

"How do you suppose it got there?" asked Thena.

Lilly shook her head from side to side, slowly. "Don't know."

"You don't think he's back already, do you?"

"I doubt it. If he was, you would know it."

"You don't think he was the one who cast the spell on that painting, do you?"

Again, she shook her head slowly from side to side. "I doubt it. He hasn't been that subtle in the dealings of his that I'm aware of. He's more like a 'here I am' kind of guy."

"Well, aside from someone trying to kill me a few days ago, I haven't seen any indication he's returned. We really need to find the pictures and get the men out. And we need to do it quickly."

"You're right about that. Maybe, you should call Fox and see what's going on."

She did, and reported that she and Lilly had found the thieves but not the art. Fox told her in return that the San Marcos detective, Jack Carter had someone in custody and wanted her to identify the suspect.

"Interestingly," said Fox, "the suspect is a woman."

"A woman," said Thena more as a statement than a question.

"Yeah. You remember, the one at the 'Day of the Dead' exhibit. I've identified her, but I can't connect her to the doctored tacos. Neither can the person who was operating the food cart, a teenager trying to make some extra cash, for a guy who was ill the day we got drugged."

"So, there's no direct evidence to link her to the drugging."

"None."

"What's her name?"

"Viviane Nin."

"Really!"

"What is it?" asked Lilly, recognizing Thena's surprise, but unable to hear Fox's part of the conversation.

"The name is one that I saw on the rental unit's list of clients," Thena whispered to Lilly.

"Interesting," said Lilly.

"Anything else going on?" Thena returned her attention to Fox.

"I told Carter that you'd gone to see Marcus and would be back in a few days. He told me that he would have to let this Nin go if there was no evidence, he couldn't hold her."

"Doesn't matter," said Thena. "She's not the one who drugged us. And, if no one was trying to rape us, why did they drug us?"

"Good question."

"On another matter, when does that 'Day of the Dead' exhibit close?"

"Why do you ask?"

"Because it occurs to me that maybe it wasn't us, but maybe there was something in the exhibit that whoever drugged us didn't want us to see. "

"So, they just wanted to get us out of the way?"

"Yeah, something like that."

"It couldn't be our two pictures."

"No. It was something else. Another picture, or perhaps a piece of sculpture, or some craft project."

"I'll find out when it closes."

"I'll bet the real person who drugged us has already left town."

Thena turned to Lilly.

"By the way, how do you know Lucifer?"

"I've run into his work in the past." She scoffed. "Let's just leave it at that!"

———◦《◉》◦———

Thena put the thumb drive into her laptop and began to scroll through the list of client names for the facility.

"There it is!" she exclaimed and pointed to 'Nin'. "Unit 167, down a few doors from the boys."

"You want to go look in it?" asked Lilly.

Thena nodded yes.

Getting back into the facility and opening the unit was no problem for Lilly. And, it was empty, except for some marks on the floor that suggested that the paintings had been there not too long ago. And there were some plastic peanuts in the corner of the unit.

"Looks like this is where the boys moved the pictures before we could get to them."

"But why would the unit be in Nin's name and not their own? What's the connection?"

"Don't know. But if we keep digging, I bet we'll find out."

"I think we need to find out much more about this Nin person."

———◦《◉》◦———

That evening Thena and Lilly met Fox for dinner in San Marcos at a restaurant called Los Vega. After some small talk, Thena asked Fox what she had found out about the exhibit.

"It closes tomorrow," answered Fox, "and some of the art has already been removed according to Susan Brown, who curated the show. She mentioned, just coincidently, a well-known curator in the area named Nin, who had some extraordinary oils in the exhibit."

"I asked her what was so extraordinary about the work."

"The palate she said … the colors were very rich. To quote her, 'It's like eating a very rich piece of pumpkin pie.'"

"I asked her if the pictures were still there and she said 'she thought that Nin had already removed them.'"

"So, Nin is well-known," said Thena. "Good. Maybe we can google her?"

"Brown gave me a catalogue from the Mexic-Arte show in Austin and pointed me to two pictures that she thought were special. Here, I'll show you."

Fox reached into a briefcase she had been carrying and pulling out a catalog, turned to a page marked Vivian Nin.

Thena and Lilly stood and crowded around Fox to get a good look. The first was titled *Old Fool* and showed a very old man with a cane walking through a very lush but foreboding forest. The second was a picture of Jesus on the road to Calvary pointing to the figure of a person who looked very much like the same figure in *The Disobedient*.

"Is that your Wolf?" asked Thena.

"Looks like him," replied Fox.

"What's this picture called?" asked Lilly.

"Justice," answered Fox.

"Ahh, it depicts the Wandering Jew, that's him being carried away by the angels. You know the story of Ahasuerus, the person who allegedly threw stones at Christ on his way to the cross?"

They both shook their heads no.

"Well, the story goes that a man mocked Christ on his way to the cross, and Jesus told him that he would be doomed to wander the Earth until he returned."

"It's just a folktale," said Lilly.

"Probably, but people in the 1300s believed it, and that figure shows up again and again in literature and art, interpreted and reinterpreted … probably hundreds of times. The real question is why the painter made the man taunting Christ look so much like Wolf?"

"You don't think that he was the wandering Jew, do you?" asked Lilly.

"Are there other pictures with the face of Wolf in them?" asked Thena.

"There could be hundreds of variations," realized Fox sadly.

Both Lilly and Thena sighed deeply.

"Questions for you," said Lilly, looking directly at Fox over the margarita glass.

"Like what?" she asked.

"Like when and where did you meet him and how you seemed to know that it was him trapped in *The Disobedient.*"

"Someone used his face for the wandering Jew, probably copied hundreds of times. But the man in this picture is not as striking as that of the person in Dore's series of etchings, where the face is so sharp featured. None of Gustave Dore's etchings look like the figure here," said Thena.

"So where did you meet him and when," repeated Lilly.

Fox sighed deeply. "I met him in Algeria, specifically Oran in 1944, during an outbreak of Bubonic Plague. He was, he said, a cleric and protesting the city closing down the churches. Those who were scared could not seek consolation and the bodies were piling up. The city was burning them to try to control the spread of plague."

"Why were you there?" asked Thena.

Fox shrugged. "Because of World War II. He said he was too. I left Spain after German and Italian planes bombed Guernica in

1937. What got me the most was the murder of innocent Spaniards, including poet Ferdinando de Lorca. The Nationalists, probably actually the Communists, apparently lined him up and shot him, along with several others. They simply randomly gathered all the males in a village and shot them, whether they favored one side or the other. No one has ever found the grave."

She paused gathered her breath and then continued. "I am a being capable of long life and I appreciate art and poetry, but I'm not immortal. And, I'm not stupid. I didn't want to take the chance of getting gathered up in some war I didn't care about and killed."

"So, you left Spain for Algeria, not expecting to encounter the disease."

"Yes. Had I known I would have gone someplace else. Wolf was quite vocal about how the city handled the plague problem … said he had been through it before."

"Oh, when?" asked Lilly.

"Don't know. One of those many plagues that ravaged Europe."

"He's that old!" remarked Thena, astonished.

"Even older," said Fox. "We shared a lot of values, got close, and then he just disappeared one day. Through the past several years, I've come to miss him greatly. I've never really found anyone else quite like him … his humor, his compassion."

"How did you come across the painting?" asked Lilly.

"Morgan and I were at an art auction a few years back, and I thought I recognized him. I tried to buy the painting then, but since I wasn't sure, some other person outbid me. I tracked the painting for several years and when it ended up in Ft. Collins, I decided that was the best place for it. Out of the way, in a small gallery. So, I just left it there."

"Are you sure it's him?" asked Lilly. "I just find it improbable that a person could somehow end up in a painting."

"Oh, it can happen," said Thena. "Like you, I wouldn't have

believed if I hadn't seen it myself. But then I find it hard to believe that you've been around for so long," she said to Fox.

"So, what's the connection between Nin and the Zuliaka brothers?"

"I can answer that one too," said Fox. "Seems the brothers visited the exhibit last week. They were looking for art, saw those two pictures by Nin and tried to buy them. But she wouldn't budge on her price, and they eventually bought two lesser pieces."

"So, they were trying to be cute when they rented a unit in her name?" said Lilly.

"Or maybe they were just being mean," said Thena. "In any case, we need a plan to retrieve the pictures."

"Got one," said Lilly. "As I see it, we need to do three things. First, we need to find out as much as possible about Nin. Fox, can you check back with the exhibit curator, Susan Brown, and see if she knows anything else. Thena, if you could check with the brothers to see where the tracking devices could have been placed on the pictures... probably on the frames, but ask if they remember seeing anything. Simple, but effective devices could have been purchased at Target or Walmart and placed on the frames. Once we have some more information, I'm going to see if the devices can still be tracked."

"How are you going to do that?" asked Thena.

"Talk to the cops ... in my new persona – Shelby Duncan, Houston City police officer."

"Won't someone catch on?" asked Fox.

Lilly smiled and then took a sip of her margarita. "Maybe, but the police want to believe and to help a brother cop. The people I pretend to be are real. I've got descriptions of them and badge numbers. I can even say y'all. Shelby is from New Orleans." And she drew out the last syllable like she really was from New Orleans.

"We've got to move quickly," she added. "If the pictures get moved again, we may never find them."

The other two women nodded.

Then Fox pulled her cell phone out of her purse and dialed the number for Susan Brown. "Since we're all in San Marcos," she began when someone answered.

"Hi," she said. "This is Hannah Fox. We spoke yesterday about a woman you identified as Vivian Nin."

There was a long pause and someone else obviously came on the phone.

"Hi, Hannah Fox here. I have some questions about Vivian Nin," there was a brief pause, "sure, I could meet you tomorrow. Lunch at Olive Garden. Sounds fine. See you there at 11:30. Your name again … Williamson?"

After Fox hung up the phone, she explained to the other women that Susan Brown had passed the phone off to a Detective named Williamson.

The women got out their phones, and started gathering information.

Fox met Detective Williamson the next day at the Olive Garden on South Lamar. She was a bit overweight, but attractive, and she was dressed nicely in white slacks, a white blouse, and a green blazer.

After they exchanged greetings and ordered lunch, Fox asked, "Can you tell me anything else about Miss Nin?" Before Williamson could answer, she quickly added, "my friends and I are trying to locate two paintings that were hijacked from a van parked at a motel and later abandoned at a rest stop off of I-10. We have reason to believe that though she was not the one who took them, she is the person who now has them. It's important that we find them as quickly as possible. They may be key to us saving two men who were kidnapped and are in danger of being murdered." She lied about part of her story, but if she told Williamson the truth, she was certain that the Detective would have her committed.

"Are the authorities looking for them?" asked Williamson, as she turned Fox's story over and over.

"Yes, the Texas Rangers, but art theft is not a major issue for them. They've got actual murders to solve and they're understaffed. So, my friends and I are helping them by following up leads."

"These are not the paintings that she hung at the 'Day of the Dead' exhibit, are they?"

"No," admitted Fox. "These are different paintings. Two oils."

"So, what were they called?" asked Williamson, as she took out a small pad and a pen.

"One was titled *The Disobedient,* and it showed a bearded man being carried off by what appears to be angels. The second picture is *Astride a Horse of Winter,* showing an Indian with a blanket over his shoulders trying to make it home in a snow storm."

"Do you know who painted them?" asked Williamson.

"*The Disobedient* was unsigned, but *Astride a Horse of Winter* was by a Canadian artist who lived with the Indians for a period. His name was Robert Woods, quite a prominent artist in his day."

"Thanks. That will help. Any other information you have will also help."

"I'm really interested at the moment in Nin. What can you tell me about her?" asked Fox.

"Well, she hung two oil paintings at the Exhibit, one called *Justice* and the other called *Old Fool.* And," she continued, reaching into her purse and pulling out a sheaf of papers, "this is a copy of the information sheet that she filled out. Homeland Security, you know." She handed it to Fox, who scanned it carefully.

"Permanent address San Francisco, born in Syracuse, New York, works as a museum curator … do you know anything about the artists?"

"One is current, a Jennings Booth, and the other an Italian I never heard of, or saw referenced, Giovanni Como. Booth lived in West Virginia. Como lived in Venice, in the sixteenth century. The odd thing about the Booth picture was that the old guy depicted appears to have no face. He is wandering through a very deep forest. When I asked Nin about it, she said that it was a perfect picture for a 'Day of the Dead' exhibit because if you look closely, you can just make out a skull where the face should be."

Fox nodded.

"I looked," said Williamson, "and she's right. There's just the faintest hint of a skull under what appears to be a painted over face. I asked Nin about it and she said that it was faceless when she purchased it. I asked her why she would buy a painting without a face and she said that it was by an artist that she knew. I interpreted her remark to mean his work, since the painting was done in the sixteenth century."

"What about her personally?"

"I checked with the curator of the Mexic-Arte exhibit and she confirmed my impression of her – very intelligent, suspicious, cold, and abrupt. She needs to control things and people. She seems to know what she wants and insists on getting it."

Fox sighed. "Did she give you any indication of where Nin was headed next?"

"She mentioned San Antonio, but she didn't say why or where specifically."

⸻ ⸳⟨●⟩⸳ ⸻

Thena hired a small plane, flew to the Preston Smith International airport in Lubbock, and rented a car. She talked to Marcus before she left and he told her about a strange night before the robbery. He was sure that someone had been both in his room and in the van.

When she asked what made him think that, he explained that things were not in their regular places. For example, he always left his car keys in the right front pocket of his pants, and he was sure he had done exactly that, but when he woke in the morning, they were on the night stand by the telephone.

Somewhat panicked, he pulled on his pants, grabbed the keys, went to check the van. To his relief, the pictures were still there, but he was sure they had been slightly moved because of marks on the van floor. With the new information from Marcus, Thena decided that she should look for information about the tracking devices in Lubbock, since the brothers had been no help.

Her car arrived in the Walmart parking lot. The whole way there, she had rehearsed the details of Nin's description: tall, willowy, with long, blonde hair, and deep, icy eyes. She also had a small scar over her left eyebrow.

At the electronics counter, a young man with a face, heavily scarred from acne, checked his records and found that no one had bought more than one tracking device. And once Thena described Nin, he said that he had not seen anyone that matched Nin's description. Most of the sales, he said, were to women who thought their husbands were cheating on them, and apparently there was a lot of that in Lubbock.

So, Thena got back into her car and drove to the closest Target store, which happened to be a few miles down the road, on University Drive, only a few miles from Texas Tech.

There, a young female student told her that the week before, a woman matching Nin's description bought four Zoombak units. She remembered her not only because she was strikingly beautiful but also because she also purchased the service plan for two months each and paid cash, almost $280 plus a $30 activation fee for each one.

"Unhappy spouses," the female explained, "usually only buy one and put it into their husband's car. I joked about her having four cheating boyfriends but she never cracked a smile … just looked at me with those narrowed blue eyes and a frown. I tried to chat her up by telling her that she was very beautiful and looked like a college student. She frowned again, pulled a wad of cash out of her red Vera Wang purse and told me to put 'em in a bag. I did."

Thena thanked her and left.

As she was driving back to the airport, she realized that Nin knew about the paintings before the Zulaika brothers stole them. How did she find out and why not just steal them herself? Then, it hit her, Nin wanted to find out where the paintings were going and probably if Pico Eyler had actually hired Val and Dani. So, if that was true, why did she steal them from the storage unit?

⸺◈⸺

Le Fey leveled the Glock 22 at Tanaka, who was sitting in the green chair by the picture window, the river in sight. On the sofa beside her were the Venus and Helix statues. Le Fey sat at a desk in front of Tanaka with Raven's *Book of Shadows* open in front of her.

"Why are you holding me at gun point?" asked Tanaka. "I offered to help you willingly. You don't need a gun."

"I do want your help, but you wouldn't come here where I have the elements and I want your undivided attention."

"I saw no need to drive here."

"I couldn't carry the Venus and Helix around in my car. They're too valuable."

"In any case," chuffed Dreaming Woman, "you don't need the gun. What exactly do you want me to do for you?"

"I want you to teach me how to work spells with the two elements here on the sofa." She pointed to them, and complained.

"I haven't been able to get any of the spells I've tried to work. I've gotten nothing and I don't understand why."

Tanaka laughed softly. "How long have you been in this world? A long time I bet." She said answering her own question.

"So?"

"So, you should have already learned that all books of spells are coded to their owner's language and dialect, even to the owner's intonation and other language features. Each book is quite unique and unless you apprentice yourself to the owner, it's unlikely that any spells you get from the book will work. The elements only provide power. You can suck energy from them, but they remain a part of nature. You can't eliminate them and you can't change them."

"Oh!" said Morgan crestfallen.

"Now," said Tanaka beginning again. "What else you don't know is that a master spell caster needs neither a verbal cue, a spell from a book, or the elements. He, or she, can operate without any of these. In truth, there are only a few beings, good enough to do them without these other aids. The only exception I know of is *The Book of the Horned God*. It will make anyone who uses it extremely powerful."

"Does such a book even exist?" asked Morgan.

"I don't know, I've never seen it, only heard of it. But I've never seen an atom or a molecule either."

"So, what does it do?" asked Morgan.

"Don't know exactly. But I've heard that it draws energy directly from the Earth's magnetic field. I've also heard that it can be focused by a master spellcaster."

"Humm. What's in the book?" asked Le Fey.

"A few spells ... very complicated. Not nearly as many as in a witches' *Book of Shadows,* but substantially more complicated."

Le Fey thought for a few moments. "So," she began, "if I want to use this book, I need its owner."

"More or less. If you want to become really proficient with it, then yes."

"And you can do nothing for me?"

Tanaka nodded yes.

"Can't you cast a spell on me that would grant me all sorts of spell casting powers?"

"You are a foreign being here, just like me, which means you already have many powers. You just haven't learned what they are and how to use them. I guess you've been indulging yourself. Instead of giving in to your whims, you need to explore yourself. I spent a long time learning what my powers were and what I could do with them."

"Like what?" asked Morgan.

"I don't know. You are essentially different than I am. Otherwise, I would recognize your signature. So, whatever powers you have, are different than mine … in kind and in strength. Spells wear out over time, they can be blocked, they can be altered, they can be countermanded. Powers wane with age, even disappear sometimes. Nothing stays the same forever. We can live a long time, but we're not immortal. Even we must die eventually."

Le Fey sighed deeply. "I don't know that I believe any of that."

"Suit yourself."

"Prove it to me. Do something spectacular. Prove it!" she insisted.

Tanaka shrugged. "Like what?"

Le Fey thought for a moment, then seized upon an idea. "There," she began, pointing to the Venus on the couch, "make her come alive!"

When Tanaka hesitated, Le Fey continued. "Don't you have a spell for that in the book?" Then without waiting for answer, she leafed to the back of the book spread out in front of her. "Tina Wakefield was very thorough. She not only indexed each spell she cross-indexed them. Here," she said, placing her finger down on the proper general category "'Bringing Life to Inanimate Objects.' She even has subtitles.

On page 150 is a spell for animating things, like people." She thumbed back to the correct page as Tanaka gestured if she could approach.

Le Fey waved her over and then pointed to the correct spell.

Tanaka read it over and then turned to Le Fey. "You understand that I have to translate this into my native tongue to make it work, don't you?"

Le Fey nodded yes.

"And you understand that even if I do translate it successfully it may not work because the pitch and intonation levels may be off slightly."

She nodded yes again.

Tanaka read the spell over several times, then began to say the translated lines to herself almost in a whisper.

Le Fey listened carefully especially for pauses and the length of them.

Then Tanaka began, softly, slowly while pointing her left-hand palm up at the Venus statue.

> *"Ooh nah, pa ta ooh nah,*
> *way, so ooh nah ta*
> *pah ooh nah*
> *sim so tey han oh to*
> *sim to mah voh oh*
> *sim sah way so*
> *to doh way."*

She repeated it again, carefully enunciating each syllable, her voice rising and falling sometimes almost two octaves.

Le Fey watched in fascination as the statue began to fade in and out, then expand, and finally to reassemble itself as a beautiful, slim, tall variation of Tanaka herself. Le Fey stared because she was naked and her genitalia were very prominent. She smiled at the two women, quite unconcerned about her nakedness.

"What mistress?" asked the statue, her smile never fading.

"What is your name?" asked Tanaka.

"Why Suisstanaka," she replied. "Do you need me for some reason?"

"No, my dear. I just wanted to prove to my friend here that you exist in a form other than the one we customarily see you in. You may go back now," said Tanaka, pushing the girl form away with her right hand, palm towards her.

"You try now," said Tanaka turning to Le Fey. "Let's see how much you have learned. Here is the spell in English. You try."

Tanaka reached into her purse and pulled out a sheet of paper with writing in pencil on it.

Morgan began very tentatively.

> *"Women are often weary.*
> *Women are often lonely.*
> *So, come to us now*
> *To talk and make friends.*
> *To share your experience.*
> *To share your joy.*
> *Come to us now."*

When she finished, Le Fey looked eagerly towards the statue, but nothing was changing. There was no fading in and out, no shower of sparks. The Venus remained a statue.

"Why didn't she come alive?" she asked puzzled.

Dreaming Woman shrugged, "Perhaps, your pitch levels, pauses, or intonation were off. The spell was written in modern English, so you need to find out from its owner how to do it. Listen to her, then copy her until you get it right."

Le Fey sighed. "Your casting worked beautifully. Was it in your native tongue? I didn't recognize it."

Tanaka nodded yes, "But few people speak it any more. It was Puhulu. From an area of Tahiti. It's akin to Hawaiian."

"Do you have a book of spells in that language?"

Tanaka smiled slightly. "Of course."

"So, you're telling me to do what?"

"I'm telling you nothing. I'm simply saying that if you want to use that," she pointed to Raven's Book, opened on the table, "then you probably need to go back to the owner. Listen to her and ... copy her voice."

Le Fey breathed in sharply, resigned to returning to Colorado. "I guess then I should take you back to San Marcos."

Tanaka nodded. "I would certainly appreciate it."

❦

Though it was late November the temperature was in the low 80's. The three women sat at a picnic table on the outside patio of the Texas State student union in the shade of some cottonwood trees with a perfect view of the San Marcos river, sipping Dr Peppers.

Once Thena returned from Lubbock she provided the information she had gathered to Lilly who was able to figure out from the police how to hack into the tracking devices.

"We need to get to get the pictures now," said Lilly, "before they're moved again."

"Agreed. And it should be easy if we act quickly," said Thena. "They're in a gated, ground floor condominium in San Antonio, called Alamo Heights, northeast of the city. The condo is owned by Vivian Niniane."

"But if its gated, how do we get in?" asked Fox.

Lilly smiled. "Think about it. Emergency vehicles, like ambulances, get in, service people get in, from plumbers to pool cleaners. Most of the people leave at sundown. But the gate codes are amazingly simple, one-two-three-four, or zero-zero-zero-zero. Or, we could just drive in when the gate is open and wait until the gate guard goes home."

Thena watched Lilly explain how easy it would be to crash a gated community, and smiled. Lilly certainly was smart … and beautiful. No wonder she was such a successful thief. And she wondered if she was kidding when she said that she would bed her at the airport. She knew what Michael saw in her. She was feeling warm all over, and she suddenly felt a flush of embarrassment.

"Amazing," remarked Fox, clearly surprised. "You know, I never really thought about it."

"So, since we know someone who lives there, our cover, if we need it, is that we came to evaluate art that Miss Niniane wants to sell," said Lilly.

"Works for me," remarked Thena.

"Shall we go today?" asked Fox.

"No better time."

They arrived at Alamo Heights at 4:30 and at the Evergreen Community at 4:45. They stopped at the guard post and identified themselves as art appraisers from Stephen A. Austin college. Lilly told the short, pudgy man at the gate that Miss Niniane wanted them to meet them at her condo to look at some paintings she had recently purchased, that she now wanted to put up for auction.

The guard tugged at his mustache, puzzled. "No one told me," he said. "Usually they let me know if someone is going be in here after dark."

Lilly shrugged. "Beats me. All I know is that we are supposed to meet her at 5:00. She'll be mad if she learns that we got stopped at the gate."

"Okay, okay," conceded the guard, and then added, "I do remember seeing a van going to her condo a few days back. Didn't know it was carrying valuable art."

All three of the women gave him their best smiles and he smiled back as he turned to raise the gate. They waved to him as Lilly checked the address on her phone, and swung around a nicely landscaped retention pond. Beyond that was the outdoor swimming pool with a clubhouse, a playground, and a restaurant, the Peter Piper. It also had an outside patio looking down on a nine-hole golf course.

"What if she's home?" asked Fox.

"We'll just tell her we were looking for someone else. We'll make up a name ... how about the Mitchells ... to evaluate some art they wanted to sell. It's best if we don't get too far away from our cover story. Then we'll get back in the car and go down to the Peter Piper and drink on the patio. Then, we'll eat and wait. Eventually we'll go back to her condo and rob the place. If she's still there, I have a surprise for her. Thena will be waiting outside with her pistol. She won't have to shoot anyone. In fact," she said to Thena, "you should unload it just in case."

"Don't worry. I never travel with it loaded. The mere thought of it going off accidently scares me."

"Won't the guard be looking for us to come back out?" asked Fox.

"They never pay attention to who goes out, only to those coming in. And if we hang out long enough, he will have gone home. He'll set it so you will only be able to get in through that entrance if you have the gate code," said Lilly.

"How do you know such things?" asked Fox.

"I'm a thief. It's my job to know!"

When they rang the doorbell, they didn't expect anyone to answer, but to their surprise, Nin opened the door. She was tall, willowy, blonde, and beautiful. But her most striking feature was her deep blue, icy eyes.

"What do you want?" asked Nin curtly. "I was just about to go out and get something to eat."

"Oh," began Lilly. "I'm sorry. We must have the wrong house. We're looking for the Mitchells. We work with Amy Mitchell and she invited us to a small party to celebrate her husband's birthday."

Lilly continued when she saw Nin frown skeptically "Do you know them? Maybe you've seen their daughter … on the playground perhaps. She's about twelve years old … blonde, lean, very pretty, like yourself."

Nin smiled slightly at the compliment.

Before Nin could object, Lilly whipped her cell phone out of her jacket pocket, and holding up one finger for silence, pretended to place a call.

"Amy, it seems like we have the wrong address." Lilly pretended to listen. "Ok, see you soon," and hung up.

Lilly gathered up Fox and Thena and ushered them toward the car as she repeatedly apologized to Nin, insisting she didn't know how they ended up on the wrong street.

When they were out of ear shot, she turned to the other's, "I guess we come back later."

They ate at the little café on the patio, under an umbrella, drank a German Riesling, and waited.

"What's the plan?" asked Fox when they had paid the bill and left.

"Two of us go in, provided she's not there. The other stands watch. You still have your pistol?" Lilly asked Thena.

Thena smiled, reached into her purse, and pulled out the gun.

"Then, let's get on with it," said Lilly.

When they pulled up in front of the condo, they waited a few minutes to see if the lights came on.

"It looks like she's gone," said Fox.

"Then, let's go," said Thena.

"Just hold on," said Lilly. "She may have baited a trap."

"Why would you suspect that?" asked Fox.

"Because I'm a thief ... and I think like a thief."

"Do you think she recognized us when we went to her door?"

"Well, she's smart and she's resourceful. And she knows she has something that we want."

"The pictures?"

"Yes, the pictures."

"So, what do we do?"

"Fox and I will go in. You wait. We'll call you if it's clear. And," she added, "bring your pistol."

Lilly and Fox made their way to the back of the condo, where a slider opened on to a community retention pond.

"We'll go in through the slider," whispered Lilly. "You can carry one of the pictures by yourself, can't you?"

Fox nodded yes.

"How are you going to get through that slider without breaking the glass?" she asked.

"I'll show you a trick," said Lilly with a gleam in her eyes.

She watched as Lilly pushed in and up on the glass, then pulled out, and the door slid out of its track.

"Believe it or not, I learned that from a cop. But that's a long story for another time," she said, as she turned towards Fox and smiled. "Slip your hand into the crack between the glass and the frame. I'll do the same. On the count of three, pull the glass towards you."

She counted in a whisper, and on three they pulled and the glass came out.

"I have my flashlight," she said as they laid the glass from the door against the outside wall and entered.

They had only taken a few steps when the overheads came on.

Nin sat in a chair in the breakfast nook, with a Glock leveled at them.

"Come in, come in," she said. "I expected you much earlier."

Lilly shrugged. "And we expected you would be gone by now. We were obviously wrong."

Nin nodded. "You really didn't think I was that dumb, did you? After all, I did see you"– she waved the gun at Fox –"and your friend at the 'Day of the Dead' exhibit."

Fox and Lilly looked at each other mystified.

Nin snickered, "I'm a shape shifter. I was at the exhibit entrance. I really expected such intelligent women to figure me out!" Nin leaned back in her chair, "So, you came for the art?"

"Only the two pieces you stole," said Fox.

Nin studied them for a few moments, then she stood and walked over to them.

"You knew that I was here, and you knew I wouldn't give you the art," said Nin. "Yet you came any way. What are you up to? And where is that other woman?"

"All in good time," began Lilly. "I didn't exactly know you were here, but I suspected you would set us up. I knew that you wouldn't exactly talk to us voluntarily, but I wanted to talk to you … to find out why you wanted the art."

"Why do you want to know that?" Nin asked haughtily.

"Because things don't make sense to us. We wanted to know

what's really going on," said Fox. "And why you took the two pictures from the Zulaika brothers?"

Nin looked down at her feet self-consciously. "I really only cared about one of them, *The Disobedient*. I recognized Ignatius Wolf as the person trapped in that picture. I wanted to free him because he has information that I want … change that – I need. He's an old friend. I've been looking for that picture for a long time. I didn't know the title, only that he disappeared from this plane very quickly."

"So, what is it that you need from him?" asked Lilly.

"It's private and personal," she said.

She looked over at Lilly. "I heard about you," she began. "You're a very cagey lady. And, a superb thief."

"One of the very best," said Lilly with a slight smile.

"But I don't know if I should accept a compliment from you."

"It's okay," said Fox. "We know some about you too. And it doesn't matter what you know about us. It won't matter."

"Really. And why is that?"

"Because once we get the pictures back, we move on. There's a person in each of the paintings under a spell. We need to get them out before they are damaged," said Lilly.

"Funny," said Nin, "that's exactly why I wanted *The Disobedient*. Are you telling me that there is also a person in *Astride a Horse of Winter?*"

"Yes," said Lilly.

"So why did you try to kill me and the other girl?" asked Fox.

"I didn't," replied Nin.

"Then who did, who tried to kill Fox and Thena?" asked Lilly.

Nin shrugged, being very careful to keep the Glock on the two women. "I have no idea. I just know it wasn't me. Why do you think it was me?"

"You just told us you are a shape shifter. And, it would have been easy for you to change your appearance. Plus, we know that the Zulaika brothers had a unit in the storage facility under your name."

"So, you put two and two together and came up with five, to quote an old cliché?"

"More or less," said Lilly.

"I really don't know what you're talking about. Who are the Zulaika brothers? And why would they have a storage unit in my name?" asked Nin.

"Don't know, but the brothers are two, small-time, Basque criminals from Idaho. They stole the paintings from us and you stole them from the brothers," said Fox.

"Never heard of them," said Nin

"If I am assuming correctly, these are the same boys that wanted to buy your pictures at the 'Day of the Dead' exhibit. They probably thought they were being cute when they took out the unit with your name on it."

"That's pretty juvenile."

"Yeah, it really is, but they are what, they are. So, what in the exhibit didn't you want Fox and Thena to see?"

"Okay. You're right. I didn't want Fox or the other girl to see the painting I hung of the old, bearded man with no face, in the woods. But I didn't drug them."

"Why would that bother anyone?" asked Lilly.

"Because one of them might have seen the man before."

"Where?" asked Lilly.

"In Paris, several years ago" was the reply.

"So, who is he?" asked Lilly.

"A friend ... and lover," she added.

"Why would it matter if one of them recognized him?" asked Lilly.

"Because he's the one who convinced Michael to go home. And, he gave him a book to custode."

"I see. Merlin, right?" mused Lilly, "He broke up my ring of thieves."

Nin nodded yes.

"Even if we had seen it, it wouldn't have made much difference," said Fox.

"And what's your connection to Merlin?" asked Lilly.

"He was, and has been, my mentor," she added.

"But you were not the person who drugged Fox and Thena?"

"Nope. I was not."

"Drop your gun!" came a voice suddenly from behind Nin.

Nin turned and found Thena with a pistol leveled at her.

"Well, I should have suspected that you were around somewhere."

"Indeed," breathed Lilly, glad to not be under the gun any longer. "We thought that you were tracking the pictures to find out who hired the Basques."

"I was. I would really like to know. Stealing art isn't their kind of crime. So, I figured someone else hired them to steal it."

"They told us it was a man named Pico, the same person who cast the spell that trapped Michael."

"That's what I heard too," said Nin as she laid her Glock on the small table next to the couch.

"But you don't believe it?" asked Lilly.

"No. It would be out of character for one of his group to stoop so low. I've never met him, but my people believe he is one of the most powerful wizards ever, a member of the Sons of Light, a magician who would just take what he wants without all of the manipulations that we have seen here."

"And you were really going to try to help Wolf?"

Nin nodded yes as Thena walked over to Lilly and handed her the pistol.

"She wouldn't have shot you," said Lilly, "but make no mistake, I will."

"So, what now?" asked Nin.

"We'll be taking the two pictures that you stole from the Zulaika brothers … and," she added, "*Justice*, the one with the repainted Wolf figure in it."

"I guess I have no choice," said Nin. "But, let me ask you a question, how are you going to get the figures out of the pictures?"

"Dreaming Woman," answered Lilly.

"Can she do it?"

"Don't know, but we've got nothing to lose. So, where are the pictures?"

She pointed to the hallway behind her. "They're down there. Second door on the right."

With her free hand, Lilly beckoned Thena and Fox over to her, and leaning in, whispered something to them.

Then, while Thena and Fox went down the hall to retrieve the pictures, Lilly held the Glock on Nin.

"I've been thinking," she began. "If you truly meant the pictures no harm, and if you want to get someone out of one of them, you can come along with us … or you could just tag along … as long as you promise not to obstruct us in any way."

Nin thought about it for a few moments, then nodded yes slowly. "That's mighty generous of you, considering."

"Deal?" asked Lilly.

"Deal," affirmed Nin.

⸺«◉»⸺

She was awake when she heard the door to her room click open and someone enter.

"Thena, are you awake?" came a whisper. "It's me … Lilly."

"Come in," Thena whispered back. "Sit," she patted the side of the bed.

Lilly sat down.

"I heard you milling around and I've wanted to talk to you for quite a while."

"So," began Thena, before Lilly had a chance to speak. "You offered to let Nin tag along with us. What were you thinking?"

"Simple. You've heard that old saw about your friends … you know, keep your friends close, but keep your enemies even closer. If she's telling us the truth, there's no foul, and if she isn't, we'll be able to find her quickly. Let's just see what she'll do."

"Okay," said Thena, a bit reluctantly. "But neither Fox nor I trust her."

"Noted!" said Lilly.

"Now what did you want to discuss with me?"

Lilly breathed out a huge sigh. "You know that Michael can't just quit making love to me. He can't. Even if he wanted to. He can't stop."

"Are you telling me that you're some kind of a witch that has cast a spell over him," she said angrily.

"No, no, no. Not really. It's nothing I do consciously. But I do have a kind of power. I just have this ability to make whoever I sleep with, better … to bring out the best in them, to cause them to evolve."

"So, it is a kind of power. And you believe that."

Lilly shrugged. "I guess."

"Where did you get it? I mean where did it come from?"

"Don't know. I only know that I'm not like other super-beings here. I'm different."

"Did it come from your parents?" Thena kept probing.

"Don't know that either."

"I thought your Mom was a French art professor and your Dad a Romani."

"Not sure about that. That's what I tell people, but I really don't know who my parents are. They, the other Romani, say that I was found along the road. Someone once told me that I reminded them of the Nuns in that ancient classic, *Gilgamesh*."

"Don't know it," said Thena.

"The Nuns were religious, in their own way, but they civilized others through sex. And now I believe them. The drive is strong in me. I've tried my best to resist it, but can't."

Thena suddenly felt Lilly's hand on her thigh, and a feeling like electricity rushed through her body. It was pure lust ... and had nothing to do with love.

———— ((()) ————

"I've wanted you from the first time I saw you ... in Paris, oh so many years ago," said Lilly as they sat, half naked, drinking coffee after it was over. "Now you understand why Michael can't resist me. I don't understand this ... whatever you want to call it, this talent. And I can't help myself either."

"I do understand," said Thena. "It *is* a kind of power. And I don't understand it either."

———— ((()) ————

When they got up for breakfast the next morning, Lilly met Thena and Fox in the Denny's dining room with a frown.

"What's wrong?" asked Thena.

"Nin's gone. Apparently got up in the middle of the night and left. The desk clerk told me she got a phone call about two a.m., and left."

"Any idea where she went?" asked Fox.

"No. I asked the clerk repeatedly if she had left a message, and he found nothing."

"Did she take her picture?" asked Thena.

"Nope. I checked the van, and it's still there."

"Very strange," said Thena.

"Yes," echoed Fox.

"So, if she left her painting, she must want us to go ahead and see if Dreaming Woman can extract whoever is in its art," said Thena.

"Do you think it really is Wolf?" asked Fox.

"Don't know," said Lilly. "But, if we go through with having Dreaming Woman extract the person, we'll find out."

"We should do it any way," said Thena. "It's awful to be imprisoned in the art, and we should help whoever is in there."

"I called Dreaming Woman last night. She's expecting us."

"Then let's eat and go as soon as we can."

"Agreed."

⸺◦《◉》◦⸺

An old woman sat duct taped to a yellow chair in the dining area of a bedroom suite on the second floor of the Residence Inn at the San Antonio airport.

"Please Viviane," she pleaded meekly. "Let me out of this prison."

Nin stalked angrily in front of the woman, who began to sob. "I can't help myself. I just can't."

"Oh, shut up you old fool. I told you what I want, and I'm not releasing you until you tell me what you told Michael Holland in Paris."

"He doesn't know anything," protested the old woman.

"That's not what you told me a week ago. And you said on the phone when you called last night that you were ready to talk. So, I practically killed myself getting here only to discover that you still were holding out on me."

The old woman looked down at her feet and sobbed. "I just told you that because I wanted to get you into bed."

"You couldn't wait until I got back?"

"No!" she replied emphatically. "I needed you ... wanted you."

"You lecherous old goat! You've used me for the last time. It's my turn now and I'm not releasing you until I've gotten all your secrets. Then, maybe I'll simply disperse you."

"That would be exceptionally cruel," protested the woman softly.

"Damn you!" erupted Nin. "You used me! Don't you feel any guilt or shame! You acted against the common law and my wishes. I was a mere child. And you stole me from the Druid priests."

She stopped and stared at the woman.

Then, she melted. "What did you say to Michael Holland ... I want every word of it, understand."

"Then will you go to bed with me?" she asked.

Nin chuffed, clearly torn. Finally, she said. "I can't bed you looking like a weird old hag."

"Then change me back."

"Alright," said Nin. "But first tell me!"

"Honest, I just told him he needed to go home, that Lilly and her cousins would eventually all get caught ... including him. That's all, I swear!"

"Okay. You swear that's the truth."

She nodded yes.

The van with the paintings arrived at the Hilton in San Marcos two hours later. Thena and Lilly found Dreaming Woman in the bar eating quiche and drinking white zin. They left Fox with the van to protect the pictures. Dreaming Woman recognized them immediately.

"Well ladies, it's good to see you. Do you now have the paintings?"

"Yes," replied Thena.

"Once we explained to the person who had them what we wanted with them, she was quite willing to give them up," explained Lilly. Dreaming Woman turned away, smiled slightly, and took another sip of her wine.

"Perhaps, I'm better off not knowing any details."

"Perhaps," said Lilly.

"I'm almost done with my quiche … late meeting … and I can take my wine to my room. Why don't you go get the pictures and bring them up to 223?"

A few minutes later, Lilly, Fox, and Thena, each with a crated picture, knocked on Tanaka's door.

A few minutes more and they were uncrating the pictures in her sitting room.

"There," said Fox, pointing to the figure being carried away by the angels in *The Disobedient,* "is Ignatius Wolf."

"And beside him in *Horse of Winter* is my partner and fiancé Michael Holland."

"What about the third picture?" asked Tanaka. "Who is in it?"

"Not sure," remarked Lilly. "But it looks to me to be a duplicate of Wolf. Maybe it's just a coincidence, but if it isn't, it looks enough like him to be his twin."

"I hope not. If it is another picture of him, then we might have a problem."

"How so?"

"We might get two Wolfs or we might get an incomplete person. I don't know. I don't understand how it works exactly."

Lilly pondered the problem for a few moments. "So, we could get back a person who has problems?"

"That's an alternative. Do you still want to extract Wolf from both pictures, if in fact, the other one is also him?"

"Don't know," said Lilly. "What do you think, Fox?"

"Have to think about it. It could be a disaster."

"Let me examine each picture in greater detail. Maybe it'll tell us something."

All the women nodded okay.

Tanaka moved up to each picture and ran her fingers over it. When she was done, she sat down on a couch in front of the coffee table, and first sniffed and then tasted her fingers.

Finally, she spoke. "Two of the pictures are cloaked in very heavy spells."

"What do you mean?" asked Thena.

Tanaka sighed deeply. "What I mean is that each of those is complicated by a mass of spells."

"Can you free them if we go ahead?" asked Fox.

"Or, do you know how we can do it," added Thena.

"Is there a simple way to counteract the spells?" asked Lilly.

Dreaming Woman shook her head no slowly. "There may be one, but I don't know it. The two complex spells were cast by masters, and woven intricately, one on top of the other. I did detect a signature here though, perhaps by a Son of Light"

"A Son of Light? What's that?" asked Thena.

"As far as I know, a group pledged to maintain the balance in the universe. They are sometimes called The Lords of Light and each one of them is a master alchemist and superb spell caster. Two of these pictures had spells cast by the same person, but I can't identify him, or perhaps her. And the spell in *The Disobedient* is cast over a series of older spells by other people. That complicates things severely. The *Horse of Winter* spell is by only one person and is a much simpler, somewhat naïve casting ... not to mention that it's a lot newer."

"Isn't there a master book of spells somewhere that we could use?" asked Fox.

"Maybe," said Tanaka. "I've heard one mentioned, a shadow book called *The Book of the Horned God.* It's supposed to be a compendium of master spells, but I don't know if it actually exists or where to find it if it does. And I don't know if it could help us."

At the mention of the *Book,* Thena glanced at Lilly, but she wasn't going to mention that they had come across it is a storage facility, so she also didn't.

"Horned God?" questioned Fox. "Does that mean what I think it does?"

Tanaka shook her head yes. "Probably. More than likely it's dark side stuff."

"So, can you free the man in it?"

"Don't know. It has been damaged. The angel on the right has been painted over and the right arm and leg are in a different position than in the original. What you can see is not his."

"How can you tell?" asked Lilly.

"When I felt the picture, I could feel remnants of the earlier picture beneath the paint."

"What does that mean?" asked Lilly.

Tanaka shrugged. "I don't know exactly."

"So, are you telling us there is nothing you can do to release the figures caught in the paintings?" asked Fox.

"Not by breaking spells." She paused. "Though, I do have another idea that might work."

"What's that?" asked Thena, disappointment edging her voice.

"A Ghost Dance," she replied. "It is a dance of resurrection, and even though it is directed at restoring the Earth, it might do more."

"Can you arrange such a thing?" asked Lilly.

"I know some Adai Caddo Indians who might be willing to try it."

"Will you ask them?" asked Fox. "We have money. We can pay whatever they ask."

"If they do it, they probably won't take money … money would make the dance impure and negate its effect."

"They do dance demonstrations at their cultural center in Louisiana, by special arrangement, but they usually won't do the Ghost Dance for someone outside the tribe."

"Why is that?" asked Thena.

"Because the dance is too sacred. Still," said Tanaka, "I have known them to bend the rules for very special occasions. There are a few Indians here at the conference. I could ask them."

"Explain our problem to them and ask if they would try it for us … and the people who are trapped in the art," said Thena.

"Tell them we can give them other things … whatever they wish," added Lilly.

"Okay," said Tanaka. "It never hurts to ask."

"And if they say yes, ask them what they want," said Lilly.

"Maybe there are variations of the dance that they could do for you."

"What might they want for such a favor?" asked Lilly. "If they want some huge payment, we would need time to prepare it."

"I do know of an instance where they agreed to do a special dance. All they wanted in return, since it was for a noble cause that they believed in, was for the recipient to plant a thousand trees in a local National Forest."

"Seems reasonable," added Thena.

"We'd be under a lot of pressure to do that fast," said Fox.

"There are two Adai Caddo men here to represent that tribe. One is Tejas and the other Cadodacho."

"Can you reach one or both of them tonight?" asked Lilly.

"Yes," said Tanaka, looking at her watch. "I'll try. Anything else I can do?"

"Yes," said Fox. "Can you tell us what you did for my sister, Morgan Le Fey?"

Tanaka sighed. "She's way too pushy. I told her if she wanted to use a white witches' book of shadows, then she needed to get that for whom the book was coded to help her, that I could do nothing. I tried; I really did. And nothing happened."

———※◎※———

"So," began Nin breaking into a broad smile after several minutes of trying to get the older woman to talk, "I'll make you a different deal."

"What's that?" asked the older one sheepishly. "I hate this prison you put me in."

Nin spoke deliberately, weighing her words carefully. "I'll free you so we can have sex, on one condition."

The old woman beamed lecherously. "Okay. Anything, you want. You must be really horny."

"I am," admitted Nin.

"You haven't had sex with me for a long time," said the old woman.

"True" Nin began to nibble on the woman's ear "… but, assure me that you told me all you know about Michael Holland's time in Paris."

"I said I did. Have you ever caught me in a lie?" the old woman asked.

"No," replied Nin.

———※◎※———

"Three thousand trees … three thousand trees," she repeated. "That's incredible. It will take us a long time to do that," protested Fox.

"It was a take-it or leave-it deal," explained Tanaka.

"And a hundred volunteers to clean up the highway five miles in both directions around their cultural center in Natchitoches, Louisiana. Wow. That's a lot!"

"As I said, it's a take-it or leave-it deal. This is a great favor and an intrusion on their beliefs."

"We'll do it," said Lilly.

"Good. Because I already told them you would."

"How soon and where?" asked Thena.

"Because they want it to remain secret, we'll have to go to their center. It's a long drive, so we'll leave tomorrow and do it the next morning. They need time to make arrangements."

"Like what?" asked Fox, then explained that she wasn't being antagonistic or ungrateful. "I ask only because I was thinking that we might be able to help them some way if we know what they need."

"You could help them gather people. The Ghost Dance, if done properly, needs several people … who are true believers. Tejas and Cadodacho wanted some guarantee that even if the dance fails to do what you want, you will at least honor your commitment to plant the trees."

"You've got it," said Lilly.

———— ◆ ————

Nin had the old woman naked and lying on the bed.

"I'm sorry. On second thought, let me re-tape your hands to the posts," she said. "I want to leave your hands looser. The sex will be more interesting that way."

"Okay," said the woman, "but you have to release me when we're done."

"Absolutely," said Nin with a snide smile.

She duct-taped the old woman's wrinkled wrists to the posts, slipped off her panties and bra, and then, paced slowly at the foot of the bed ... back and forth as if she were in a shooting gallery. She glanced now and then at the woman on the bed and frowned.

"You're just too ugly to have sex with," she said finally. "I just can't bring myself to do it."

"But you promised!" protested the woman. "You promised! I'll do whatever you want. Just make me happy!" she murmured almost in hysterics.

Nin shook her head slowly back and forth. "Hold on! I'm not backing out! I just think the whole business could be more appealing ... and more fun."

The woman quieted and looked puzzled.

Nin moved her hands slowly in a series of gestures and she chanted almost under her breath.

A few minutes later the old woman's body burned with a low blue light and began to change shape. A few more moments passed while Nin whispered a spell with her eyes closed. Then, she opened them and looked down. A handsome young man with a short black beard, a sparkling smile, and deep green eyes greeted her. He was also well-muscled.

"There!" said Nin. "That's how I remember you... as a handsome young man." She snorted lowly. "Aren't you glad you taught me that spell?"

"Now we'll both enjoy this a lot more!"

⟞⟐⟝

Sunrise two mornings later, they stood in a field that was part of the cultural center. It was very secluded, and in the middle of a circular clearing, there was a tall, old pine tree. Its lower branches were covered with strips of different colored cloth, claws, horns, stuffed bird replicas, and large feathers, perhaps of an eagle. Even though it was illegal to kill eagles, there was a very large underground market for their feathers. The Indians collected them when they saw them. Each of the items hanging from the tree was an offering to the Great Spirit.

Eighteen Native Americans had gathered including Tejas, who was their medicine man and Cadodacho, who was their chief. The women, nine of them, wore loose, robe-like dresses with a triangle of blue at the neck. The rest of the dress was painted with sacred symbols: moons, suns, stars, and sacred birds. Each had a feather tied in her hair at the crown. The men wore ghost shirts, painted similarly and each had what appeared to be an eagle feather in his hair.

Both men and women had painted their faces red. The women had a black, half-moon on their foreheads, the men the same on one cheek.

Tejas and Cadodacho wore buckskin pants and shirt, and the chief had a full headdress. In front of him was a fire pit, metal and full of glowing coals, and on its grill were candles of various scents: juniper, pine, and magnolia in particular.

Three paintings leaned against the trunk of the tree.

The dancers formed a circle around him, the tree, and the paintings. They then began to circle in a dance with Tejas chanting,

> *"Father, I come.*
> *Mother, I come.*
> *Brother, I come.*
> *Father, give us back our friends*
> *Who have been entombed in*
> *These paintings without*
> *Their consent."*

As they chanted, they grabbed hands and spun faster and faster.

If one fell down, they left him, or her. After several minutes and repeated chanting, Tejas signaled them to sit down where they were and to continue to chant softly. Six who fell down seemed to be in trances.

They repeated the dance at noon, then again at sunset.

Finally, as the sun was about to duck behind the horizon and Tejas had begun another chant with "Father, I come," the paintings began to radiate a soft blue light, and as if by magic two men appeared from them, looking disheveled and disoriented.

The third painting, *The Disobedient*, shimmered in blue. They watched it curiously for several long minutes, but then, the blue faded and it remained as it had been.

～◈～

"Keep going! Make me happy!" screamed the willowy blonde astride the smiling young man.

Her eyes were closed. She moved and screamed again, "Make me orgasm, like you used to do!"

Then her body went rigid, she shrieked once, and collapsed on him, eyes closed.

He smiled.

Both breathed heavily.

Finally, with a deep sigh, she rose and made her way to the bathroom. He rested. When she reached the door, she turned and made a gesture. As she closed the door, the young man's body glowed bluish and transformed back into the old, wrinkled woman it had been.

She tried furiously to free herself from the duct tape that held her wrists and ankles to the bedposts. Finally, she gave up, and began to sob softly to herself.

"Oh, be quiet, you old fool," said Nin when she returned from the bathroom. She had a washcloth in one hand and a small towel in the other. She began to clean him up. He sobbed softly. Then, she transformed him once more and paraded in front of him.

"Remember this," she said as she walked back and forth, pausing at each turn so he could take in all of her attributes. She was still stunningly beautiful.

She bent over him and began to run her tongue over his stomach. He started to become erect again. Then, she climbed back over him and made it once more. Finally, she fell across him exhausted.

Finally, with a deep sigh she rose. "Well, that takes care of my problem and frankly I don't care about yours." Another gesture and the old woman appeared again.

"Are you going to un-tape me and let me out of this damned spell? You promised me," pleaded the woman.

"Are you going to tell me what you said to Michael Holland because I know you didn't tell me everything?" she countered.

"Okay, okay, okay," sobbed the old woman. "It was an August day in Paris and very hot. I arranged to meet him at a little café on the left bank. He told me he was worried because the jobs were getting more dangerous and Lilly's cousins were becoming more careless. He wanted to know if he should just up and leave before they all got caught. Like you or me, he couldn't turn her down. She had a way about her, not just with men but women too. He was torn. He wanted to stay with her, on one hand, but he knew that what they were doing was wrong. He asked me what he should do. I told him, he should run away from her as fast as he could. He should not even go home and pack anything. He should just go. He knew it was just a matter of time before all of them got caught. And he couldn't stand the thought of jail."

"So," said Nin, who slipped on a red thong and sat in a chair at the end of the bed, "did he?"

"Yes, he went straight to Orly, bought a one-way ticket and caught the next flight for New York."

"Did he know who you really are?"

"I don't think so. I'd met him five or so weeks earlier, Lilith introduced us. And I managed to run into him several times in the intervening period. When I detected that he was worried, I asked him why he seemed so sad, and eventually he told me he was worried about Lilly's cousins getting caught and blaming him as the brain behind the robberies."

"And what else?" she asked.

He hesitated.

"Come on," she pleaded. "You're holding back something. I can tell."

He sighed. "I didn't want to tell anyone about this. And, in fact, if I give you the rest, you have to promise that you won't tell anyone else."

She considered his request. And then countered with, "I could just leave you in that old woman form for a long time ... or until you get sick of it and tell me anyway. I can wait you out, you know."

He was suddenly angry. "Okay! If you want to play a waiting game, then I won't tell you! I can be just as stubborn as you can."

She waited, measuring his resolution. Ten minutes passed slowly.

Finally, she said, "Okay. I was just testing you ... to see how important this was."

"Okay," he began, "it's about the book."

"Of the Horned God?"

He nodded yes.

"I was looking for someone to take it off my hands. A lot of beings knew about it, and several wanted it. A few were at the game where I won it from Lucifer; others heard about it from them. The word was spreading. Admittedly slowly, but spreading nonetheless, and I was afraid someone would get it into his head he could take it from me. And I was afraid they might use you against me, to tell them where I had hidden it."

She snorted. "Ha! So, you were worried about me?"

"Well, yeah!"

"Common," she began again. "You bet me in that 'Devil's Ride' game. You certainly weren't worried about me."

"I had a plan." He explained.

"And what was that?"

"I would outcheat him. I always was pretty good at cheating and he had been winning big pots all night. My plan was not to change my cards, but rather his. And I did, and it worked. He was really surprised when he turned over his cards, and discovered that his flush was lower than mine."

"So, you wagered me against a book."

"Not just any book, but the seminal book of the greatest spellcaster ever."

"Seems pretty risky," she offered.

"Yeah. But in the end, Lucifer outwitted me. I was so confident, so sure I had bested him."

"What do you mean, he outwitted you?" she asked.

"He gave me a false book."

"He did! How could he?"

"I'm not sure," said Merlin in his cracking, old woman's voice. "But I've finally come to believe that he somehow altered the spells that were in the book ... not all of them, and not in the same way, but enough to make a difference."

"What makes you think that?"

"Because through the years, when I've tried them, some – the simplest – worked, but the more complicated ones didn't. No matter what I did. I even got a recording of his voice, practiced it until it sounded perfect, but it didn't matter, I still failed. So, what he gave me was not the true *Book*."

"And after all these years you still haven't figured out what he did to the book?" she said as she crossed and uncrossed her legs … slowly so he could see her.

"Nope. I've tried everything I can think of."

"And yet the book is where you learned master casting?"

"A lot," he agreed, "but not all of it. Through the years, I tried reworking some of the spells, with some success. And I created my own, but the fact that the spells from the book didn't work told me that something was wrong. Eventually, I didn't need the book at all, but I didn't want someone else to have it, and I couldn't destroy it, so I sought a place to hide it."

"Who would have been after it?" asked Nin. "Surely Lucifer wasn't looking for it, especially if he really did alter it. He was on the Grunfeld cross by then, a prison of his own making."

"Right. He didn't need it. He was already a master spellcaster, and he had no real conception that he could lose, regardless of what he said. His own egotism prevented him from the reality. But there were others who lusted after the book, some of them were at the Devils Ride games. Even though Lucifer always won, to be invited was an honor of its own."

"Where were these contests held?" asked Nin.

"You already know … in Dublin, at the Traveler's Inn. You were there with me on more than one occasion."

"Yes, I remember being there. Was that in 1239?"

He nodded yes.

"I was only fourteen years old then … and still in training by the Druids. You took me from the Skathach Philosophy."

He nodded again. "I rescued you from a life of eternal boredom."

She looked down at her feet, ashamed. She stared for what seemed awhile. Then, she finally looked up. "I guess."

"How much more of this do you need to hear before you release me from this old woman's body. You already know all of it."

"Why would you wager me for the book?"

"Because I knew I could be a better cheater than he was. And if he hadn't been so damned sure of himself, I wouldn't have tried it. He is an extreme egotist. I thought I could play on that and beat him. And I did."

"That was a hell of a chance you took with my life. Had the Druids found out, they would have killed me. I was training to be a Priestess of Vesta."

"No, no, no," he said shaking his head from side to side. "See, I know something about them that very few people know. They can be bought. I would have rushed in, so to speak, and made an offer for you. I'm sure they would have accepted it."

"Really."

"Yes. Will you release me now?"

"You still haven't told me what this had to do with Holland? Where is the book now?"

Merlin shrugged. "I'm not sure, but I think it is still in a safety deposit box in the Caymen Islands. That's where it was. I got tired of moving it around, and I knew no one would suspect Holland, so I gave him a key and told him that there was a rare book in the Caymen National Bank in Georgetown. I gave him the box number. He asked if it had been stolen, and I told him no, that I won it in a poker game, since he wouldn't know what a Devil's Ride game was. He then asked who I won it from, and I said Lucifer. He started to laugh. He didn't believe me. He thought I was, what's the current expression, pulling his leg."

"But he took it anyway?"

"Yes. He asked me again who I won it from and I told him again, Lucifer. He just thought I was withholding information."

"You really are an old fool," said Nin.

"I guess. Now, I've told you all of it. Release me."

"I don't think so," she said. "Someone has to make you pay for what you've done."

"But you promised," sputtered the old woman. "You lied to me! You're an awful person … no honor, no integrity, no loyalty."

"Maybe," she said. "But I am what you made me," and she smiled slightly.

———✦———

The sun was setting. "We can do no more," shouted Tejas to Thena.

"And it worked, Father," replied Dreaming Woman. "Thank you, thank you, thank you." She held her hand out, palm up, and then pointed to each of the three women in turn. "The Caddos have agreed to the terms, as you have."

"We already know that," whispered Fox.

"I know you know," Tanaka whispered back, "but ritualistically, it demands repeating. Kind of like a handshake to seal the bargain."

She bowed her head to Tejas as a sign of respect and urged the others to do likewise. One after another they did.

"Come on," she urged softly, "back to the lodge." She placed a hand on the shoulder of both Thena and Fox. "Someone will bring the two men with them in a few moments. They will give both men clothes and clean them up. At the lodge, we will celebrate with coffee, beer, or tea, and sandwiches. This has been a very successful day for the Caddos, as well as us."

"How so?" asked Thena.

Tanaka hesitated. "I'm just guessing, but this may be the first time they have used the Ghost Dance to restore more than just the Earth. So, it'll be a revelation to them, and they'll be excited about its possibilities."

"Why would they do it?" asked Thena. "I mean, their rules are so strict."

Tanaka smiled knowingly. "I have powers of my own … different than most, but powers nonetheless. I wish to speak no more of it. Come, follow me!" she ordered.

The three women followed her into the lodge where they acknowledged several women who were sitting there with a nod, some who had participated in the Ghost Dance. They took seats at the east end of the room in front of a roaring fireplace and waited.

When Tejas and Cadodacho entered several minutes later, each had a rainbow- colored umbrella over Michael or … Wolf.

Two women took the umbrellas. Two others guided the men down a long hall. And Tejas and Cadodacho plopped themselves down in overstuffed chairs in front of the fire with a nod to each of the women who had petitioned the Dance.

"Will they be all right now?" asked Tanaka.

"I don't know," replied Tejas.

Cadodacho signaled a woman who stood close by for food, and then requested a cigar. Smiling at Tejas, he asked, "Cigar?"

Tejas nodded yes. "This is an occasion. The gods are pleased. Not only did they grant our petition, they showed their pleasure by weeping." He then turned to the women and asked. "Cigars, Ladies?"

Fox, Thena, and Lilly shook their heads no, but Tanaka nodded yes.

The cigars arrived, were cut, and then lit before anyone spoke again.

"I speak for the tribe," began Tejas. "We are very pleased with the results we achieved the past two days, but I must apologize to you because we could do nothing with your third painting. I think it was too encumbered with other spells. But I'm just guessing. I really don't know. But I detected overlays of spells from several wizards, most likely the Sons of Light. But that is just a guess. Still, you have shown us light. We see that out Ghost Dance can restore more than just the Earth. And for that, we thank you."

It was dark and snowing lightly when Raven's doorbell rang. When she opened it, a beautiful red-haired woman stood before her, wrapped in an expensive coat, smiling, and holding a large, navy tote bag.

"Are you Tillie Wakefield?" she asked.

Raven nodded yes.

"I came to return something I believe was stolen from you," she said and reaching into the tote pulled out a heavy, black-leather covered book, which she pushed at her.

"Oh, my God!" exclaimed Raven as she took it. "You've brought back my *Book of Shadows!* Oh, my God! Oh, my God! I thought it was gone forever. Thank you, thank you, thank you! How —." She stopped in mid-sentence. "Come in and tell me how you got it. I'm so eternally grateful. Please take off your coat, and sit down. I'll make you some tea. It's cold out there. I've got Earl Grey, Darjeeling and English Black Breakfast tea. Or hot chocolate if you prefer. It is chilly out there this evening," she repeated.

"You must have a Keurig!" said the woman with a chuckle.

Raven nodded and then they both laughed.

"Yes, of course," replied Raven, immediately disarmed.

The woman thought about her choices for several seconds, and then asked, "Do you have any herbal tea?"

"I do. I have Lipton's Orange and Spice tea from their 'Soothing Moments' Collection. And I would be delighted to make some for you."

"That would be great," said the woman. "The drive up here from Denver was hectic, to say the least."

Raven went to the kitchen, made the tea, brought it out, and set it on the small, glass table between them. She began to leaf through the book randomly. Then noticed that the woman was watching her carefully.

"Sorry, just checking to make sure you brought me the right book."

"What do you think?"

"Looks like the right book." Raven paused as she stared at her book, greatful to see it again. "I can't tell you how much this means to me. I'm delighted to get it back. Tell me, how did you come by it?"

"Quite by accident, really. I'm the niece of the woman who stole it. But we're not real close because she's so much older than me. Though, we do get together occasionally. I was in Austin, Texas, when I found out she was in San Marcos, just a few miles from where I was. So, I called her."

"And you two got together?"

The woman nodded yes. "We had a few drinks and she told me about the book. She had me try to cast several of the simpler spells because she wanted to see if it was just her or if something else was going on. I couldn't get them to work either. She was terribly frustrated. When I failed, she threw the book on the floor in disgust and ordered me to take it out and throw it in the Colorado River. I told her I would, but --"

"You didn't. You brought it to me. How did you know to bring it here?"

"Your name and address were on the inside cover."

"Oh yes. I had forgotten that I did that. Well, I thank you again. A lot of work went into it, work that would be impossible to duplicate. How can I reward you?"

"Well, honestly, I had an ulterior motive," she said as she sipped her tea. "Once I had time to examine it and appreciate what it was, I had an idea."

"And what would that be?" asked Raven.

The girl looked down at the floor shyly. Then, she suddenly looked up, "I was wondering if you would teach me how to cast spells?"

Raven considered her question. "I would love to, but I have a problem. I run a coven, and it must always have no more than thirteen white witches. We do only good work, nothing bad. Nothing to hurt people. Unfortunately, there are no openings at the moment. So, I can't officially include you."

The girl looked disappointed. "Oh, that's all I would want to do … good work. Help the world be a better place."

Raven smiled. "You sound a little like you are answering a question in a beauty contest. I'm sure you believe what you say, but fixing the world is no easy thing."

"I was hoping …"

"Let me think about this for a while. There might be a way."

The girl looked up at Raven and smiled hopefully.

"What is your name, my dear?"

"Marie, ma'am. Marie Le Fourbe."

"Are you French?"

"No, but my grandmother married a Frenchman in World War II. She was a nurse in the Red Cross."

Raven smiled sympathetically. Then she rose and began pacing slowly. Finally, she stopped and placing her hand on the girl's shoulder, announced, "I'll tell you what. You seem like a nice, sincere girl. I can't let you into the coven right now, but you can become an adjunct member … preparing eventually to be an initiate. If you accept that role, you can come and study with us."

The girl beamed.

"Will that be all right?"

"Yes, ma'am. Thank you so much."

"Do you have a place here in town."

"Not yet. I've been staying at an apartment in Denver."

"You might want to move closer. The women in the coven all live nearby."

"Of course," said Marie. "I thought I would move here if you accepted me. I really want to learn how to use that book." She nodded towards the leather covered book now on the table between them.

"May I ask you a question … a personal one?" asked Raven.

The girl nodded yes shyly.

"How will you support yourself if you move here, to Boulder?"

"You mean moneywise?"

"Yes."

"I'm a Trust child. I get a regular stipend monthly. All I have to do is notify the trustees where to send it. But I thought I might also work some. I especially like the new libraries. I thought I might try to get on at the University. I'm very interested in learning about the new, electronic library."

"Sounds like a good idea. Maybe I can help. One woman in the coven works at the University. She could put in a good word for you. By the way, when can you move?"

"Well, I have arrangements to make and plans for tomorrow—Thanksgiving. But probably not until mid-December."

"Good. I'm calling a meeting of the coven now that the book's back. I'd like you to attend … meet the others."

"Of course."

"I'll start telephoning in a few moments. Thanks again for returning the book. More tea?"

"Sure," said Marie.

It was several minutes before Michael and Wolf appeared. Meanwhile, two men entered the front door of the lodge, each with a painting inside a large, black trash bag.

They greeted the woman with a nod and then Tejas and Cadodacho and placed the paintings at the fireplace, one on each side. Then they pulled off the trash bags. The face on each figure was blank. Only white space showed where the features had been.

But as they watched, the faces originally in the pictures gradually re-appeared.

Michael showed up first. He was smiling broadly. "I don't know what happened to me or where I was," he remarked as he pulled Thena close and kissed her. "How long was I gone?"

"It's okay," she said, gently. "We'll sort it out later."

Then he saw Lilly. "What is she doing here?"

Lilly smiled at him, turned both palms skyward, and shrugged.

"She was a great help, Michael. I couldn't have gotten you out without her."

"Okay. You can explain that to me later too."

"And," she said, nodding towards Fox, "There is Hannah Fox. You remember her, don't you?"

He nodded yes. "But who is that dark skinned woman over there?" he asked gesturing toward Tanaka.

"A very wise woman," replied Thena. "Again, I couldn't have gotten you out of the painting without her help."

Then he saw Tejas and Cadodacho. "Who are they? Wait! Where the hell am I?"

"They are Native Americans. But as I said, I'll explain all of it later."

A Caddo woman approached with a tray of sandwiches and soft drinks. She offered them to him.

"Eat, drink, Love! I'm glad you're back!" said Thena.

He took a sandwich and a glass of iced tea.

"Lemon-almond chicken salad," said the woman with a smile. "Eat. You'll feel better. Sit over there by the fire." She pointed to a chair in front of the blaze. "It's getting cold outside." She placed the tray down beside him and held out her hand.

"My name is Kitsai."

"Thank you. Thank you, all of you, for all you've done."

"It was another ten minutes before Wolf appeared, his hand being held by the same woman who had led him to the shower.

"He's warm and clean," she said to no one in particular, "but he's not in good shape."

Fox gasped when she saw him. He limped badly; his right arm seemed paralyzed, his right cheek was scarred, and he was squinting like he was having difficulty seeing.

She led him to another chair on the other side of the fireplace and helped him sit down. Kitsai approached with the tray of food. She handed him a sandwich, which he took anxiously and a cup of hot coffee, that she placed on a small, wooden table by his seat. "There's a sandwich, turkey I think, and on a stand to your right is a cup of hot coffee."

"Thank you, thank you! It seems like I've been away for a long time, but where?" he asked.

Fox approached him slowly, tears streaming down her face.

"Wolfie," she whispered. "It's me ... Hannah."

"Hannah?"

"Yes. Here, let me help you." She lifted the coffee cup to his mouth. "Slowly ... sip slowly. It's very hot."

He did as she directed, sipping slowly. "You're terribly thin," she said. "So, eat this sandwich slowly. Little bites at first." She handed him the sandwich.

He took it and ate ... not much and not fast.

"Hannah? Where have you been? I missed you." He didn't wait for her to answer. "Where are my friends? My brothers?"

"They're not here. You are among new friends. You're not in Spain, or Italy. You're an ocean, and centuries, away."

"He's punishing me ...," he said after several minutes. "I've done wrong. I've been disobedient. That's what he told me He was going to call the picture ... *The Disobedient*." His voice cracked and he brushed away a tear.

Fox leaned close to give him another sip of coffee. "I saw Him," whispered Wolf, "I saw Him."

"What are you talking about?" asked Fox.

"Him. I saw God," whispered Wolf again. "He told me he was going to punish me for not obeying Him. I disobeyed Him."

"What exactly did you do … or not do?" she asked.

Wolf seemed not to hear her.

"He told me to stay away from Lucifer, to not get gathered up in his plans, to stay humble." His voice cracked again.

"I told the fallen about the Venus and the Helix anyway, that they were not that important … that what was important was what gave Lucifer his power … that the *Book* was important. Lucifer knew it and how to use it."

"What *Book* are you talking about, Wolfie?"

"The *Book of the Horned God*, of course," he explained as if everyone in the lodge should know what he was talking about.

"But what is that?" asked Fox.

"A book that explains how all of this works," he made a sweeping gesture above his head with his arm. "How all this came to be and how it works."

"How do you know about this book?" asked Fox softly.

"The essences explained it to me." He continued on without waiting for her comment, "as well as the location of the etched copper tablet."

"Etched copper tablet?" asked Tanaka, who had been patiently listening. "I've heard of a copper tablet that was found among the Dead Sea Scrolls. Supposedly, it promised treasure."

Wolf nodded yes. "It also told all lost souls how to find their way home."

"Who are the lost souls and what homes have they been prevented from returning to?" asked Thena.

"It could mean a lot of things," speculated Tanaka.

"That's the beauty of it," said Thena, "It's so wonderfully ambiguous."

"I'm sure it's not about anything as simple as returning to other worlds. It has to be about Christian souls returning to the church … or to Christ," said Tanaka.

"Or any other religion returning to its source …"

"Like Buddha, or Brahma or some aboriginal God," said Lilly.

"So, if we don't act like a certain body of religious thinking, if you will, then we are lost souls," commented Tanaka.

"It was written by men," said Lilly, "many centuries ago. It was meant to control women and children, and anyone else who fell outside their ring of power, outside of what those who were in control believed."

"Very political," observed Thena. "So, you are saying, my way or the highway."

"Do as I say, not as I do," added Lilly.

"He punished me for telling them," said Wolf.

"Telling who?" asked Fox.

"The fallen ones."

"As long as they were misdirected, it took the heat off … a red herring. It was his own way of controlling them," said Fox.

"Give those who want power something else to chase," said Lilly. "They didn't know about the book or the copper scroll."

"How do you suppose Lucifer got the book? Do you suppose he wrote it himself?" asked Thena.

"No," said Wolf, correcting her. "He told me it's been around since the beginning of time, since the creation of God himself."

"But that doesn't tell us how he got it, even if he was God's right-hand man," said Thena.

"Maybe that's what Milton's revolt in heaven is really about," said Lilly.

"It's a Christian metaphor," said Thena. "No revolt really happened."

"But other religions pose similar rebellions, their own ways, their own metaphoric explanation for subduing disobedience," observed Lilly.

"If there really were a Book full of such lore, where would it come from?" asked Lilly.

"From some other world, like you, Tanaka, and you, Fox," said Thena. "If you and your ancestors were bumped here, maybe some book of other-universe knowledge was too," said Thena.

Everyone was suddenly quiet for a few moments.

Then, "What if we weren't bumped here by a collision of some sort, like a Big Bang ... but rather we were imprisoned here," suggested Tanaka.

"For something we, or our ancestors did in those other worlds?" asked Fox. "Maybe those who arranged to put us here don't want us back."

There was another period of quiet. The Native Americans had been listening respectfully.

Then Tejas spoke. "Does it really matter. If you could, would you go back to another, alien world, a world you know nothing about?"

The others thought about his statement for a few seconds.

"I wouldn't," said Fox,

"Me either," echoed Tanaka.

"Thomas Wolfe was right when he suggested, 'You Can't Go Home Again,'" said Thena. "Because it no longer exists the way that you knew it. The only thing that is constant in this world is change. I, and others, assume that principle is the same in other worlds."

"Yes," interrupted Cadodacho, "our tribe recognizes that change is the only constant."

When they were about to leave, Tejas approached Thena and Lilly, "We still have the third painting. Do you want to take it with you?"

"Yes," said Lilly.

"Yes," agreed Thena. "Maybe we can find a way to release whoever is in it."

⎯⎯⎯◦((◦))◦⎯⎯⎯

Tanaka and Lilly stood on the third-floor balcony of the Southern Inn in Natchitoches shivering in the rain that had started after the Ghost Dance. It had gradually turned cold and the wind kicked up. Michael and Thena arrived, and Fox ushered them to the balcony.

"Look at him," she whispered. "He's gone over the edge."

"What's that on his face?" asked Thena.

"Lipstick! He's painted himself with it."

They looked down at the motel's swimming pool.

Wolf had taken off his shirt, and decorated his naked skin with wide red streaks.

"Like tears," interrupted Thena.

"Running down his cheeks."

"And on to the rest of his body," added Michael.

"Watch him!" said Tanaka. "He's trying to dance, to complete some pattern, but he can't."

They watched as Wolf took a step forward, as if on some rain-soaked, invisible grid that only he could see. Then he stumbled, nearly fell down, and started again. The whole time he mumbled something that was barely audible.

"He's acting compulsively," uttered Michael.

"Does anyone know what he's saying?" asked Thena.

"Not really," said Fox. "He seems to be apologizing to God for his perceived disobedience. He told me earlier today that the whole time he was in the picture, God confronted him, chagrined him for what he did. Now he's begging for understanding and forgiveness.

And," she added, "he seems to think that he has to complete some dance pattern to get it."

"An apologia pro vita sua," said Thena under her breath. "Like Cardinal Newman."

"Or," added Lilly, "like Red Skeleton's 'I've been a bad boy.'"

"The last conversation I had with him showed that he was rational, unstressed."

"What do you think happened to him?" asked Lilly.

"I'm only guessing but think about the problem. Literally … part of him seems to be missing."

"Maybe," said Thena. "There is that third picture that the Codo's could not get with their Ghost Dance. As you'll recall when we saw it, the figure being carried away, looked like Wolf. What if someone painted another one of him but didn't follow the first pattern. Much the same physical position, but not quite."

"A variation. I'll bet that's it!" said Lilly.

"But a second capture of his DNA. Maybe some apprentice painter trying to imitate the master, whoever that is … maybe used a brush that the original painter used without thoroughly cleaning it."

"The picture looked damaged, on Wolf's right side," said Fox.

"So," said Michael, "we need to find out some way other than a Ghost Dance to release him from *The Disobedient* painting."

The three women nodded almost as one. "Not going to be easy!" said Thena.

"Oh, oh!" said Tanaka. "Someone better go down and get him. He just stumbled and fell down, fell over his own feet. We all need to help him!"

"I'll go," said Michael.

The Book of the Horned God

Michael and Thena sat at the rooftop bar atop the Frenchmen Hotel. It was sunset and the Mississippi glowed orange. Thena swizzled a stirrer in her Tanqueray and Tonic. Michael thumbed the salt ringing the glass of his Margarita.

"It's great to have you out of the art," she began, "even if your insertion was accidental."

He smiled at her then looked down at his drink.

"I don't think I can really explain how nice it is to be free. I can only imagine what those that the Sons of Light have imprisoned must feel after a while."

"So, what was it like ... really?"

He thought for a few long seconds before he answered.

"Well, I never lost consciousness," he began, "though there were times I wished I could have." He shrugged. "I played games mentally, with you ... chess and scrabble, even War. But that got old fast since I was not only playing for myself but you too. So, I tried writing stories and even poetry. But I found it hard to finish anything if I couldn't write it down."

"I didn't know you wrote poetry."

He nodded.

"I dabbled."

"Will you show me some?"

"Eventually. I need to rework it first. Writing poetry and fiction is hard. I kept going over different ways to say things. It wasn't like my articles for R. B., that was a straightforward argument. Easy writing, not like making up characters and whole worlds. I taught myself a trick," he added.

"What's that?"

He smiled. "I imagined I was at a beach … on the Gulf. It was my private place. No distractions, no interruptions. Every time I went there, it got easier."

"That's quite a trick."

"I guess. It was easy once I learned to keep other things out."

"Oh," she said disappointed.

"Not you," he hurriedly corrected. "I thought about you a lot. In fact, thinking of you really kept me going."

"And Lilly?" she asked.

He sighed. "Yes," he admitted after a time. "I did think of her often."

"Good," said Thena.

"Really? Why is that?"

"Because she and I became quite friendly while we were trying to figure out how to get you out of that picture."

"Well, to be completely honest, it's good that the two of you became friends."

"I couldn't have done it without her," admitted Thena.

Michael shrugged. "Whatever it takes. And when I think of her, I remember that old guy in Paris, Merle DuBois, who warned me about her and her cousins. 'They'll eventually get caught,' he warned. And they did."

"But the police didn't get Lilly?" she questioned.

"No. You know why?"

"No," answered Thena.

"Because she was the one who turned them in."

"Really? Why would she do that?"

"Don't actually know. She can be vengeful. But I suspect it was because they were always bugging her about me not being a Romani and she got tired of hearing it. Bear in mind that I don't know if that's actually true, especially after they got out of prison, they thought I turned them in and kept the money from a theft we had just pulled. She actually placed my share in an account in the Bahamas and gave me the interest. I took it but I felt guilty. She told them what she had done, but they didn't believe her. Any way you can't mention that I told you. You can't breathe a word of it."

"Why would I tell her?"

"She swore me to secrecy. I know that you two got friendly when I was in the art. I don't want you to slip up in a weak moment. If she thought I told you, it would change her relationship with you. And, I don't know if that is important to you."

"It is. So, my lips are sealed to quote an old cliché," she said sarcastically and pretended to zip her lips closed and throw away the key.

"Come on," she pleaded, and reached over and placed her hand on his. "Give me a poem … just one."

"Okay," he finally conceded. "The only one I remember well I call the 'One Legged Gull.'"

The one-legged gull
Floats above the deck
On southerly breezes
Off the Gulf.
I wonder, does she
Float forever
Or does she land
To work the parking
Lot at IHop.

Thena laughed in spite of herself.

"Cute," she said. "You made that up."

"No, no," he protested. "It really happened. Once I saw a gull with only one leg from a balcony on the Gulf. And I remembered it."

"Sure," she said doubtfully.

They stared at each other for what seemed a long time.

"I missed you … and I was afraid I was never going to get you back."

"Me too. I thought at times there was no way out for me."

He smiled over at her.

"And there was that damned snow hitting me in the face again and again."

She chuckled.

"How about another round?"

She nodded yes and he stopped a passing waitress and ordered more drinks.

———•((•))•———

Azza tugged at his beard and frowned. He was sorry now that he folded.

Maybe, he thought, he could have bluffed his way through and won. He had three deuces.

No, he said to himself, no one ever beats Lucifer. The best a person could hope for was a close second. The pot was largest of the night, maybe a hundred thousand credits.

Baal, who was shorter and clean shaven, watched intently. He was sure that Lucifer often won by trickery, but he dared not challenge him. He was, after all, the leader. Besides Baal enjoyed the company, so if he bet low, he would just look like he was being conservative. He had no intention of claiming that Lucifer cheated.

Astaroth, whose hair reached below his shoulder blades, dealt two cards to Lucifer, who picked them up and smiled. He dealt only one to Merlin.

"Let's make this interesting," said Lucifer. "I'm going to put my *Book of Shadows* into the pot. Hold on while I go get it and then I'll call." He nodded toward Merlin.

Everyone knew he was planning on Merlin folding. That was a ploy Lucifer often used in these poker games.

He disappeared while the players talked among themselves.

"Do you think he'll put his real book of spells into the pot?" asked Belial.

The other players shrugged.

Just then, Lucifer returned carrying a large, red-covered book under his left arm. It had a silver embossed satyr head on it. He placed it the pot. Then he looked up at Merlin and smiled. "What of equal value are you going to put in?"

Merlin frowned. What did he have of equal value to add to the pot?

"Only thing I can think of is that blonde girl sleeping in the loft," said Merlin. He checked his hand once more.

The men in a circle on the floor gasped.

"Niniane? Really?" asked Lucifer.

Merlin nodded yes. Like the others, he was tired of losing to Lucifer. Besides he was holding what he considered a potentially great hand.

"Wow," said Belial, "she was in training by the Druid priests who tend the Temple of Vesta."

"And I stole her and reeducated her in the ways of sexual pleasure."

"She ought to be great in bed," said Astaroth.

"She's better than great," emphasized Merlin. "I trained her myself."

"She's certainly lovely," chimed in Azza. "I would take that bet."

"Okay," said Lucifer. "Okay."

"Lay out your cards then," said Merlin.

"Each lay down your cards one at a time," said Astaroth. "Let's make this interesting. You start," he said nodding at Lucifer.

Lucifer laid down a queen of clubs.

Merlin followed with a king of hearts.

Lucifer then played a ten of clubs. Merlin followed with an Ace. Lucifer followed that with a jack of clubs and Merlin followed with a ten of hearts. Lucifer then played a nine and Merlin a Queen of Hearts. Lucifer played a seven of clubs.

"Lucifer has a low flush," announced Astaroth. "And you potentially also have a flush in hearts."

Merlin breathed a deep sigh and laid down his last card. It was an ace of hearts.

"My goodness!" said Astaroth, pointing down at Merlin's cards. "He's got a royal flush ... in hearts."

Lucifer stared down at the cards, pretended he couldn't believe it.

"Okay," he said finally. "I'll be damned. No puns intended. I guess you've beaten me."

Trembling, Merlin reached for the *Book,* but Lucifer reached across and placed his hand over Merlin's.

"You've got to give me time to copy it," he said.

Merlin nodded. "Certainly, my old friend. Six weeks enough."

Lucifer mumbled yes.

<hr/>

Later that evening Lucifer and Astaroth sat in front of a log fire drinking ale.

"I was surprised you let Merlin win your book," said Astaroth.

"Yes, that was a bit of bad luck," said Lucifer.

"Come on. I felt the magic in the room. I think you let him win." Lucifer smiled knowingly.

"Didn't you want that icy-eyed blonde?"

"You heard him," began Lucifer. "She was in training with the Druid priests who tend the Temple of Vesta. After I thought about it, I didn't want to spend years watching out for them, and besides, Merlin trained her himself. He bragged about it. I can only imagine what he taught her. No. I decided that she was damaged goods. So, I let him keep her. And it gave me an opportunity to have Paolo make several copies of *The Book*."

Lucifer smiled sheepishly and shrugged. "Maybe, I changed a card or two in his hand."

When Dani and Val Zulaika reached their room, they were soaking wet. It was raining harder and there was a steady, cold wind from the north.

Val shrugged. "It wasn't raining when we left," he protested grudgingly.

"But the weather channel predicted a storm this evening."

"Guess they finally got it right." Val chuckled to himself.

"If you hadn't insisted we stay for Bingo, we could have gotten back before it got too bad."

"But Bingo is really the only gambling you can do in Texas, unless you can find a high-end, private poker game. And I did win a thousand dollars," added Val.

The brothers were so intent on blaming each other they failed to notice the tall, thin man standing in front of the slider.

"Who the hell are you!" demanded Dani when he saw the man move out of the corner of his eye.

"I'm the person who hired you to steal those paintings from the old professor."

"Oh, Mr. Pico" said Val suddenly recognizing the man they met in the library.

"You haven't kept up your end of the deal," said the man.

"We weren't going to give you the stuff until we saw the cash," said Dani.

"Yeah. We don't know you. How can we trust you?" added Val.

"I gave you a cell phone number to call when you got to Austin with the pictures."

"You did," said Dani. "And I did right after we put the paintings away ... but there was no answer."

"Then," said Val, "someone else stole them out of our storage unit."

"What!"

"Yeah, right out of the unit." Val continued, "When we went to check on them the day after we put them there, they were gone!"

"So, there was no point calling again," added Dani. "We've been thinking about how to get them back."

"We checked with the old guy at the gate. He said the only other car that'd been in was a dark blue Buick Enclave, that came in right after we did."

"I remember that car. That blonde lady followed us down to our unit but drove past when we stopped."

"She said 'Howdy boys' and smiled at us as she passed," said Val.

"She certainly was beautiful," added Dani, "certainly was beautiful," he repeated. "And," he added, "she had the most remarkable icy blue eyes."

"Where did she go?" asked the man.

They shrugged.

"Weren't paying no attention," said Val.

"I was," said Dani. "She turned down the short alley just around the corner from us."

"Did you try to find out who she was?"

"No!" replied Dani. "I didn't want no one to think I was a stalker."

"She wasn't going to think that," said the tall man, with a sigh. "She was probably after the art! My bet is she had tracking devices on the pictures. So, all she had to do was follow your SUV. Once she knew which unit was yours, she came back and stole them."

The brothers stared blankly at each other.

"Sorry," apologized Dani. "I guess that means you're not going to pay us."

The man thought about the comment and made a decision. He finally said, "I'll pay you. You did steal the paintings. And it's not your fault she's smarter than you. She's just a very smart woman, and I should have taken extra precautions. So, it's my fault, not yours."

"Sounds like you know her," said Val, his curiosity suddenly roused.

"I do," he replied, "She's been after one of those paintings for a long time."

Crow, who was taller than either of the brothers, had a narrow face, a very straight nose, a dark complexion, and a shock of grey hair, headed for the door.

"Here," he said as he passed the wet jackets the brothers had thrown on their beds, and tossed a wad of bills on the one nearest to the door. When he reached the door, he stopped.

"If you have any contact with that woman or hear information about her, call that cell number I gave you earlier." He started to leave.

"We'd be happy to do business with you again Mr. Eyler," yelled Dani after him.

Crow was still using his mentor's name, Pico Eyler, as an alias. He figured that it would be better if the brothers did not know who he really was.

Michael practically carried Wolf in. Both were soaked. Wolf was limp, semiconscious and babbling.

"Come on! Get him into Fox's room," ordered Lilly.

The women helped Holland get Wolf to the elevator, and they all rode to the third floor. Then they took Wolf in, undressed him, put him into a warm shower and into bed. He continued to mumble and remained only partly conscious.

"Should we call a doctor?" asked Fox.

"I don't think that'll help him," said Tanaka. "What will, I believe, is getting that other picture that seems to have a variation of him in it and freeing him. Fox and I will stay with him. Why don't the rest of you go down to the restaurant and figure out what to do next."

"So, you think the problem is missing essence?" asked Thena. "That even sounds funny."

"There's a bigger problem," said Tanaka

"What's that?" asked Lilly.

"Someone created that second version of him. It wasn't an accident. And that person, or group, won't be happy when they find out."

"I've got to get out of these wet clothes," said Michael interrupting the train of thought, "or I'm going to freeze to death. And, I need to think about this. I'll go change. Tejas found some pretty decent clothes for me. I'll get into them and meet you in the restaurant."

When Michael got to the restaurant, only Thena and Lilly were there.

"Where are the others?"

"Both of them thought they needed to listen and note what Wolf was saying. So, they stayed with him. They'll do room service," said Lilly.

Holland sat down. The women had ordered drinks, and he flagged down the waitress.

"Margarita. On the rocks. Top Shelf. No salt."

She wrote down his order and hurried away.

"Now," he began, "what down you make of all this?"

"Well," began Lilly, "by the way, welcome back from the land of the almost dead." She flashed him a big smile. It was a kind of tease.

He looked at her nervously and started to tap his fingers on the table unconsciously. "Thank you. I'm kind of surprised to see the two of you together ... it makes me nervous."

"We're cool" offered Thena. "I could not have saved you without her. In fact, I called her!" She shrugged. "Send a thief to catch a thief. Isn't that the old saying?"

He nodded yes.

"She is one of the best. And she's proven that the past few weeks."

"There is no jealousy," added Lilly. "I just do what I do!"

"Still," said Thena, standing and picking up her drink, "I think you and Michael need to talk." She nodded at Lilly. "I'll get a sandwich at the bar and sit by the pool." She left.

Michael felt his head swimming with images; a spider, Lilly's face on it, the web and himself a small child trapped as the spider approaches. He wiped sweat from his brow with his napkin.

"Do you want to order any food?" asked the waitress as she set down his drink. She startled him, bringing him back from his web.

"I'll have a filet, medium. A baked potato with sour cream and a salad with blue cheese on the side."

Then he realized that he hadn't given Lilly a chance to order or even say if she was ready. "I'm sorry."

"For what?"

"For jumping ahead like that. It was rude."

"No problem." She turned to the waitress. "I'll have a taco salad and I could use a coffee." After the waitress left, she turned back to Michael, "Do you have a problem with me being here?"

"Not actually." He lied. "Thank you for the bank account."

"You're welcome," she shrugged, "it was only interest."

"I appreciate your help ... I really do. And you and Thena seem to have worked out your differences."

"You seem nervous around me," she said. "Why? You didn't act that way when we set up my cousins."

"I know. You're right."

"So, what's different now?"

"You remember," he began slowly, "when I left you and the others in Paris?"

She nodded and sipped the last of her drink.

"The old man I used to have coffee with at the Bagatelle told me, the last time I saw him, that I needed to leave you and the others. I guess I let him know how much I cared for you and how much I hated what we were doing."

"Hah" she laughed, "he could have guessed that when you told him you followed me to Paris!"

"I guess so."

"But why would you tell him that we were art thieves. That's just dumb."

"I didn't," Michael protested. "He already knew. He knew about other jobs you pulled and your family. He told me, 'once a thief always a thief,' and if I didn't leave immediately, I'll be drowning; that you'll destroy me."

"That's just nonsense. Why would I destroy you? I loved you ... still do in my way."

"You wouldn't do it on purpose," he said. "It would be a consequence of who you are. 'Predatory', he called you. And the picture he painted was of you as a spider, closing in on a prey stuck in her web. That image stuck in my mind. I had that as a nightmare when I returned to New York. Gradually it went away. But lately it's returned ... before I got drawn into that picture."

"What can I say? I certainly meant you no harm. As I've said before, I love you. But I am what I am. And if you'd stayed with me you would be a very different person than you are now. That's the way the world works. By the way ... just my opinion ... but you make a much better knight in shining armor than you do a thief." She laughed lightly. "Call Thena on your cell and tell her to join us. We need to talk about that other picture and restoring Wolf!"

He did.

———— ⊸(⦿)⊷ ————

"Eat," said Nin as she jerked the duct tape from the old woman's mouth. "Eat or I will put you back in the painting."

"I don't like this old body!" said the woman. "It's fat and achy."

"That's the idea. Being in a body instead of in a picture or that crystal cave gives you mobility. And soon, if we catch up with a Son of Light, I'm going to need you to be mobile."

"Why do you need a Son of Light? You're talented ... and I certainly am."

Nin stared at the wrinkled face, chuffed under her breath, pushed a ham sandwich on a plate with chips at the woman and shook her head slowly from side to side.

Finally, "Yes, you are," she said softly. "But you are also a victim of your excesses. And," she added, "maybe some old age dementia is setting in. I've noticed in the past 100 or so years that given a chance, you will ... *will* I said ... screw things up."

"When I find a Son of Light," Nin continued, "I'll need you. Meantime, if I keep you under control you won't mess up more."

"I don't like this body!" she repeated. "And won't someone be looking for this Professor Antonelli?"

"This is not the real Antonelli, idiot! It's a duplicate of her that I shape shifted on you. And you are right, it is a prison, a different kind of prison than you are used to."

"I'll break this spell!" the woman said angrily and suddenly. "And then we'll see! I'll put you into an old man's body!"

"Go ahead if you can." Nin shrugged. "I learned all I know ... well almost all ... from you. So maybe you can break it. But you forget, when I left you several years ago, I spent time with Wolf. He taught me even more ... not so much new things, but refinements of old things ... how to hang a spell in such a maze of overcasting that it is almost impossible to unravel, except by the original caster. So, go ahead ... I'd like to see you try."

Antonelli's smile faded. She took a bite from the sandwich, then took a drink of water. "Why can't you give me some good French wine? I have a cellar full of it ... somewhere. I brought it back from France when I was last there."

"Because I want you sober. And every sip of wine you take, no matter how good, kills off some of those gray cells I'm going to need."

"No, no," she protested. "I went there specifically to bring back some of the finest wine around."

"You went there, Merlin, chasing tail, specifically that alleged beautiful gypsy thief that Koldo Orbed told you about. He put her image in your head and you finally had to go see her for yourself. And she rejected you because she was in love with someone else and so you started working on him. And eventually you, masquerading as his friend, convinced him to leave her and go back to the states. She rejected you, and rejected you, and rejected you and in a moment of complete insanity, you not only told her about *The Book of the Horned God*, your showed it to her! Hah! And she still didn't want anything to do with you" Nin scoffed. "I don't know, maybe she was afraid of you. So dejected, you decided to get even by convincing her lover, that Holland guy, to custode the *Book*. What you didn't know at the time was that it wasn't the real *Horned God Book*. Lucifer made a false duplicate and told you it was the real one. In fact, he made several I understand."

"Didn't matter" the Antonelli facsimile protested, "Lilly and Holland thought it was real, though neither knew that the other knew about it, and it diverted all those friends of Lucifer, who periodically showed up and chased after it."

"Maybe so, but like so many other times, you just couldn't stop chasing tail. You're nothing but an old letch. Then there was the screw up with the Wolf picture."

"I tried," he said murkily. "You said you needed Wolf to get the *Book* ... because he was the only one who knew where the real one was. So, I went to Paris to see the girl. Not to seduce her but to befriend her and acquire a palette knife that she had in her possession."

"What could that possibly have to do with you screwing up the Wolf business? Are you trying to con me?" she asked angrily.

"No... no. The palette knife was used by an artist she hired to repair the *Disobedient*. Her cousin Corsi stole it from a private collection but in his exiting from the estate banged it against a stone post at the front gate and tore the covering and the picture. His brothers, Sheva and Kassa hauled several other paintings out of the house. They obviously had to take the painting to someone they knew to repair the damage .... Lilly knows people."

She listened and then started to pace in front of him as she considered what he told her. Finally, putting the fingers of her right hand on her chin, "So you tried to draw Wolf out of the repaired painting?"

"Yes," he confessed.

"But it didn't work because the repaired picture was too much of a variation of the *Disobedient*, not the original."

"Yes. But if he's ever released from the original, he may act strangely since all of his essence is not there."

"Where did that variation come from?"

"It was painted from a sketch left by the original artist, Michael DeAngelo. It was common for the Master to leave several sketches or partially finished paintings for his apprentices to finish. No one knows who actually completed the work, but a couple of his apprentices went on to be quite successful."

"So, after the damaged painting was repaired …"

"… and part of it repainted," he added, "… what happened to the picture?"

"The thieves sold it back to the people they stole it from. And they were happy to get it back."

"Why would they care?" she asked.

The Antonelli facsimile shrugged like the answer was obvious and Nin should have known it.

"Well, any painting by DeAngelo is worth a couple hundred thousand dollars now. And, the owners didn't want the authorities looking into their art collection; rumor has is it they weren't obtained legally."

"So, they didn't report the theft?"

"Right."

"They got their art back but it cost them."

"Right again."

"It's kind of like buying expensive insurance."

"So, the end result is that there are two pictures containing Wolf essence, effectively preventing him from being released as his whole self. But he has to be released from the painting periodically, as all of those who are picture captives, so he won't dissolve forever into that void between worlds. And if anyone wants to get the information that he has, they need both pictures."

"Many beings have tried to obtain the *Disobedient* and release him."

"Yes, and I actually had it for a brief spell."

"You did," he said. "But releasing him is not easy. The Son of Light who originally bound him hung a very complex spell, and others laid spells on top of it. So, all those beings who tried failed."

"Well," she mused, "I guess I've been wrong. I've been trying to get to Pico Eyler. He is a Son of Light, right?"

The facsimile nodded yes again. "Why?" he asked.

"To see what limits there are on the powers of the Venus and Helix."

The facsimile chuckled.

"Why are you laughing?" His arrogance annoyed Nin.

"Well first, it's unlikely that Eyler would tell you. You're known among the Sons as a trouble maker. And second neither the Helix or Venus would give you any power."

"Why not?" she said surprised.

"Because, they only function as lenses; they only magnify or diminish powers users already have."

"Then why are dozens of people trying to get them?"

"Because, like you, they believe the ruse."

"How do you know all of this?"

"Wolf told me. He was at that poker game where I won *The Book of the Horned God* from Lucifer. That book can give you power, and it can, like the lenses magnify already existing powers. What he didn't tell me but I figured out was that Lucifer had absolutely no intention of giving me the real book. He gave me a copy. I should have guessed because it took him four months to actually turn it over."

"How did you eventually figure it out?"

"Well," the facsimile shrugged. "None of the important spells worked … only the little ones. You know that spell-casting is particular to the owner of the *Book of Shadows*. I knew that. I could imitate him perfectly, but I kept thinking I was doing something wrong. The truth dawned slowly, very slowly. I thought he was a man of his word. I would even ask him what I was doing wrong, and poker faced, he would give me some bull about this or that, and make a suggestion."

It was Nin's turn to laugh. "So, the consummate conman got out-conned." She laugher harder. "I find that very funny."

"So, where is the real book?" she asked when she got herself under control.

"I think only Wolf knows now that Lucifer has been temporarily dissolved. Lucifer wanted the game to continue because it got his greedy friends off his back and kept the book safe. And he didn't really need a book to do what he wanted to. He was so powerful that he could operate without it."

"I bet his buddies were very disappointed when he fell into a sprite trap and dissolved."

"Yep."

"So, you're telling me that we need both pictures to call up Wolf and we need him to find the real *Book of Shadows*."

He nodded yes.

"Like the other fools, I bought into the red herring."

He nodded again.

Then suddenly she flashed anger. "You could have stopped me, you know!"

"Yes."

"Then why didn't you?"

"You wouldn't have believed me if I tried."

"Well," she reflected sheepishly, "that's probably true. Don't be so smug," she shot at him.

"I'm not."

"So, what do we do now?"

"I'm not doing anything," the old lady said. "I don't need a *Book* to tell me what to do. I'm skilled enough without it. Plus, through the years, I've seen that power corrupts."

She chuffed at him, looked disappointed and stated, "I either have to make Wolf whole or find Eyler."

"Yes."

"Either way I'll need your help. What can I do to convince you?"

"Let me out of this fleshy prison," he replied. "First the Crystal Cave, then the hut in the forest, now this ... the most humiliating of prisons."

"Oh?"

"Yes," he offered. "I have to pee all the time."

"Okay," she said reluctantly. Then she made several hand gestures, and mumbled ... almost in a whisper. And the iconic short-bearded form of Merlin reformed itself.

"Now, what can I do for you? Make love to you? I'll return to that young stallion form you once begged for." He winked at her.

She smiled slyly. "I need to get that other picture of Wolf back. His girlfriend has it," she said as he undressed her.

He nodded and kissed her on the neck, "Of course."

"How do you know so much about Wolf?" she asked.

"He was at the poker table when I beat Lucifer."

"But why would he tell you secret things? He was Lucifer's friend," she cooed.

"Well, yes." He kissed her breasts. "But he was also scared of Lucifer. He wanted some insurance in case he fell out of favor. That old demon had a temper and thought nothing of betraying his companions or friends. He really only came to like Wolf when he learned that he had spat at Jesus on his way to be crucified."

"The Wandering Jew?" she asked.

"No. Not necessarily. But someone like him."

"Another one cursed with immortality."

"Yes," he said.

"So how," she began as he stripped off her last bit of clothing and gently forced her down on the bed, "should we go after the picture?" she asked softly.

"The easiest way. Ask that Fox girl for it. Don't tell her what we want to do, just sell her on the idea that this is a chance to make Wolf whole. She loves him."

Nin seemed surprised. "Do you think that'll work?"

"Don't know. And we won't know unless we try."

<hr />

Lilly first heard of the mask when she called her answering service. She found a message there from Roderigo Alvarez asking her to call as soon as she got his message, something about an item he thought she might be interested in.

She knew that Alvarez headed up a group that were, for lack of a better term, grave robbers … though she knew he hated the term and preferred to be called a liberator. So, she called.

After initial greetings, Alvarez began his approach.

"I found this mask," he told her, "in an undiscovered Incan site. It was in the Honduran jungle, completely covered by vines and underbrush. It appears to be genuine. It's a representation of the Incan Rain God, Chacmool. If it is or not, I can't say. One of my men identified it as a sky god. It's solid gold. Are you interested?"

"I might be," she said. "Let me look at it."

"I`ll send it separately."

Lilly waited patiently while Roderigo loaded the photograph.

Finally, a picture came up on her phone.

"It's certainly beautiful. Are you sure that's solid gold?"

"Yep."

"And you think it's Incan?"

"Also, yep."

She examined the mask carefully, trying to determine its authenticity. Big nose, mouth turned down at the corners, narrow but bulging eyes, and sloping forehead. "It sure looks real," she said finally. "How much are you asking for it?"

Then before he could answer, she added, "You know I rarely buy items directly; I prefer to steal them from people who have acquired them illegally. And have some sort of general insurance to cover them just in case."

"Yes. I do know, but I thought because of its rareness you might be interested."

"How do you know it's legitimate?"

"Easy," he began, "because I took it out of the site myself."

"So, you are technically speaking, grave robbers."

"Of course," he replied. "I thought you already knew that. That's what we have always done. And now with that new aerial radar, we have already seen many sites that no one knew were there."

"I suspected," she said. "And now I can't con myself any more. What are you asking for the mask again?"

"Twelve million. It is, after all, solid gold."

"I'm tempted. But you sure you wouldn't take eight mil for it?"

"Can't do it. It's just too big a prize for me to lower my price below twelve."

"I'm tempted, really I am. But ..."

"... but you can't afford it. I understand," Alvarez finished her sentence.

Then she had a bright idea. "Look, I would really like to see it in person some time. So, I'll make you a deal. If you tell me who you sell it to, I'll pay you for the information. A thousand even."

"Okay, okay. You know I'm greedy. I'll call you and tell you. I have some people who are interested."

"Good," she said. She already had a plan.

———«(●)»———

A week later, she heard from Roderigo again. Picking up the phone anxiously, she noticed that he was still in Honduras.

"Lilly?"

"Yes." She heard a heavy sigh at the end of the line. "Just making sure. When you live on the edge, caution becomes your best friend."

"Agreed. I assume you sold the mask."

"Yep. Got sixteen million for it."

"So … you've literally struck gold."

"In a sense."

"Who to?" she asked.

"A hedge fund partner named Duncan Winters. I've sold to him before. It appears that he has a secret gallery in what would normally be the basement of his home. It is temperature and humidity controlled … and paneled," he added.

He continued. "I was actually in it once, several years ago. Some 'lost' paintings and several pieces of statuary. Winters is very private. Never mentions that he has several million dollars' worth of art in his house."

"How did you get in?" she asked, her curiosity piqued.

"Well," he hesitated. "If I tell you, you have to promise not to tell anyone else."

"I promise."

"As you know, I am a thief … and a very successful one. Winters is also a thief … just a different kind. A lot of art in his gallery would sell for big bucks if he were to get caught. And he's very proud of what he has accumulated. He had to show it to someone. And I seemed safe. So, one evening he blindfolded me, took me to his home, and then, still blindfolded, took me down into his gallery."

"So, who does he share his collection with? His wife?"

"No, he's divorced now. No children. Only the few of us who are as deeply entrenched as he is. I mean, he could blackmail us if he chose. As mutual thieves, we're safe."

"Thanks, Roderigo."

"Sure."

"I'll transfer the funds right away."

She filed away the information. She would get to it sooner or later.

———◉———

Eleven of the group sat around in the fireplace of Suzie Douglas' house. In the center of the white-hooded group, was an elaborate altar. On the floor was a pentagram in red paint and a circle circumscribing all.

"We meet here," explained Raven in a whisper to the white-hooded, young woman sitting on a straight-backed wooden chair behind her, "because her basement is so nicely finished."

"We are only eleven initiates," said Douglas. "Shall we begin anyway. Maybe the two missing members can join us in session. It is snowing after all, and both are driving from Denver at rush hour."

Raven nodded yes. And the ceremony began.

"First," explained Raven who had risen a few moments earlier and now began to speak, "I want to express my deepest appreciation publicly to the young woman who came with me, Maria Fourbe, and returned our *Book of Shadows*. She would like to join our group so she can learn to cast spells. Since we have a full number, I explained to her that becoming a member would not be possible. Yet, we owe her a great deal and as I thought about it and did some research on the reason for keeping our group limited to 13, I realized that Margaret Murray is responsible for that number. There is little evidence according to Guiley's *Encyclopedia of Witches and Witchcraft*, to support that number. I suspect that 13 has become a folk tradition because of the general population's belief that it is unlucky and that groups like our coven do evil things."

She took a breath and waited for a moment before continuing, "I'm proposing that we accept Miss Fourbe into our group."

She looked out at the others. Then, "do you have any questions?"

"Does she know what we try to do?" asked Douglas.

"She's here now, Suzie. You and anyone else should take this opportunity to question her."

There was a murmur of agreement.

"Are you willing and ready to answer their questions, dear?" asked Raven.

Maria nodded yes.

The questioning from the ten woman who were present, except Raven, continued for over an hour but Le Fey, who had much experience at being tested, answered all of them with grace and a smile. She played the ingenue perfectly and when the women asked all they could think of, she had won them over. The women's questions focused on her intentions and whether she knew that as witches they only did good. And a number of the questions repeated, in different words, what had been asked before. Everyone seemed to feel she needed to participate, except Raven, of course, who had already vetted Fourbe.

Maria charmed them, and soon some of them were proposing that when the current "maiden" position became vacant, she should fill it. She fit its requirements perfectly, a comely young woman whose duties were primarily ceremonial, and who served as companion and hostess for the grand mistress, that being Raven.

She said the right words; she was interested in learning the information in the *Book of Shadows* so she could 'heal others and seek her own spiritual development.'

She could stay. She would participate as a novice.

Meanwhile Le Fey chuckled to herself as to how easy it had been to "con" them. But she reminded herself, not to be too knowledgeable, or to slip out of character.

Thena strolled into the restaurant with her drink and sat down. "Did you two work everything out?"

They nodded simultaneously.

"Then I guess we need to figure out how to fix the second Wolf picture so we can make a whole man, so to speak."

"Well, I've been wondering, Nin had all of the pictures we saw at her condo tagged with microchips so they could be tracked. If she just wanted to steal them, she already had. Why not then remove the tracking devices?" said Lilly.

"Because they were bait," said Thena in a moment of realization. "She wanted to see where they ended up. And we know that Dani and Val Zulaika were working for one of the Sons of Light. She wanted to meet him!"

"I guess so," said Holland. "That actually makes sense."

"Why would she care?" asked Thena.

"Because she wants to know how to use the Venus and Helix to secure power?" suggested Michael.

"It has to be more than that!" said Lilly. "I've been a thief all my life and I've got a feeling about this. There's more here than meets the eye to quote an old cliché."

"So, what are you thinking?" asked Michael.

"We should keep the paintings chipped and see who we catch, just like Nin was doing," said Lilly.

"And who do you think will come?" asked Michael.

"I suspect, one of the Sons of Light," said Thena.

"Then we're agreed," said Lilly.

"Will it be more beneficial than restoring Wolf's memory?" asked Michael.

Both Thena and Lilly shrugged. Then Thena offered an observation.

"I'm sorry about Wolf, but even if we make him whole, we don't know if it will be beneficial. The bigger issue is the control of the elements by someone whose motives are not in our best interests."

"And one of The Sons of Light will know more if he'll agree to help us," finished Lilly.

There was a pause while they sipped drinks and finished eating.

"And maybe he can tell me what that *Book* Merle gave me is worth."

"What!" exclaimed Lilly, startled. "What book? Are you talking about that old lecher Merle who used to bug me in Paris years ago?"

"Yes."

"He gave you a book?"

"Yes."

"What was it?" she asked cautiously.

"I don't know. He felt sorry for me because I was wrestling with leaving you and your cousins and ..." he added, "the life of crime. So, he gave me a leather-bound book and asked me to hold it for him. I didn't really look at it. And I didn't really want to be bothered with it. But he gave me $3,000 to take it, store it, and never tell him where it was."

Lilly continued to stare at him amazed.

Michael continued. "He told me he would send me money every May first to pay for it. And he's been good to his word. Every May I get a cashier's check for another three thousand dollars."

"Where's the book now?" asked Lilly.

"I don't know. I gave it to Max Stewart, my friend who was the curator of the Art Museum at the time, paid him, and asked him to hide it. I put it into a black trash bag and requested he put it in a temperature-controlled place. I give him half the money Merle sends me. He was on his way to Dallas the week after I came home with it, so I suppose it's somewhere here. He told me it was in Texas if I ever needed it. I thought Merle might want it back, but I never told Max about Merle."

Lilly was shaking slightly.

"What's wrong?" asked Michael.

"We know where that book is," said Thena who had been listening quietly. "Lilly recognized it and shooed us away from it. It's in storage in South Austin. But before we left, I noticed a silver, horned satyr outlined on the cover."

———— ◉ ————

When they got to Fox's room on the third floor of the motel, they heard a buzzing sound, which Thena identified as a hair dryer, or dryers.

It took several moments for someone to hear their knock and let them in. Tanaka pointed to two oil paintings that Fox and Nin were blowing with warm air from the dryers.

Nin, was testing the paint in the pictures to see how much heat to apply.

"Who's that?" asked Michael nodding towards the blonde.

"I don't believe it!" said Lilly in a low voice, surprised.

"That's Nin," said Thena, "the woman who stole the paintings from the Zulaika brothers."

"What is she doing here?" asked Michael.

"It appears she is softening the paint in that messed up area of

The Disobedient with carefully applied heat," explained Lilly suddenly realizing what was going on.

"Why?" he asked.

"My guess is that she's going to remove paint from *Justice* and use it to fix the figure of Wolf in *The Disobedient*," Lilly said with a titter.

"How could that be?" he asked.

"Well," started Lilly, "if some of Wolf's DNA was disturbed when *The Disobedient* was damaged and it messed him up like he is now, then we're lucky that no one was able to release him from that painting. Who knows what he would be like then?"

"How is all that even possible?" asked Michael. "I mean as far as we know, there was no contact between the two paintings."

"But if they were painted by the same knife at different times then maybe there's a connection between the variations. The understanding of Wolf's essence would exist in the mind of the conditioner," speculated Thena.

"Maybe," said Lilly.

Just then there was a knock on the door. Michael, who was closest, opened it.

Standing before him were two people, a young man with a short beard, Roman nose, and very black hair and a paunchy woman about 50.

"I'm Wylit, a friend of Vivien Nin. She asked me to find a professional art restorer and meet her here … not an easy task in a small town like this. Had to go all the way to New Orleans." He turned to the woman. "This is Margarette Frost. She works at NOMA."

"NOMA?" questioned Michael.

"Yea. The New Orleans Museum of Art. She's a restorer."

"Then, come in. Nice to meet both of you," said Michael stepping aside and gesturing towards Fox and Nin using hair dryers. "You look awfully familiar, Wylit. Do I know you from somewhere?"

Wylit looked at him carefully, feigning ignorance, then shook his head. "I don't think so." Then he joined Margarette at Nin's side.

"I feel like I've met that man before," said Michael.

"I have that feeling too," added Lilly.

She waved Tanaka over.

"How did this happen?" she asked.

"It was very strange. The blonde woman came to the door and proposed that she and Fox try to restore Wolf by fixing the painting. She said it's possible by taking paint that contained the figure from *Justice* and correcting the other figure. She sent that man," she pointed to Wylit, "to get the restorer, someone who can determine how the Wolf figure should look."

"What happens when that process is complete?" asked Michael.

"Then the restorer, Margarette Frost is going to paint the correct Wolf form into *The Disobedient*," answered Tanaka.

"As I suspected," said Lilly.

"She'll have created an allegedly complete Wolf in the picture."

"How is Nin going to release Wolf then?" asked Lilly.

"She never said, except to tell us she knew someone she thought could do it … a man named Eyler."

"So, she'd have to find Eyler," said Michael.

"Exactly, but she also said he was the one who paid the Zulaika brothers to steal it originally and she felt she could find him because of the microchip in the frame."

"Isn't he the one who put Wolf into *The Disobedient*?"

"That's what the woman said."

"So, she's right. He could get Wolf out," said Thena.

"I don't know how she's going to get Eyler to release Wolf. If he put him into the picture, he must have had a reason," said Holland.

"She says he needs to release Wolf."

"Why?"

"Someone else is coming … a creature that Eyler fears… or,"

she corrected, "is so dangerous that Eyler felt he needed to collect *The Disobedient* himself. She thinks that's the reason he paid the Zulaikas to steal it."

"Who? And how does she know this?" asked Lilly.

"She says Merlin told her. It seems that eons ago he was at a game of poker with Wolf, Lucifer, and some other fallen angels, and she says Merlin won Lucifer's *Book of Shadows* from him. It was officially called *The Book of the Horned God*. Now that Lucifer himself has been dispersed, one of those 'angels' wants the *Book*. He thinks Wolf knows where it is."

"So, he's after the Wolf pictures," said Thena.

"Right."

"So why is she here?" asked Michael directing his attention towards Nin.

"She told us when we tried to steal the pictures back from her, that Wolf has some information she needs. So, it's possible he knows something. We agreed to work together but then she disappeared," explained Lilly.

They all watched in silence as Margarette Frost, the finisher, mixed the paint from *Justice* on her palette with fresh paint and repainted the figure of Wolf into *The Disobedient*.

A half hour later, Margarette Frost stepped back from her work, looked it over carefully, made a few discrete corrections, and then corrected some more and finally announced she was done.

"Can we use the hairdryers to hurry up the drying process?" asked Nin.

Frost nodded yes. So, Nin turned the one she had been using on and spun it toward the new version of Wolf.

Wylit nudged her and she scowled at him, clearly angry.

"You'd better set that dryer on low," he cautioned her. "You're beginning to move the paint around."

She glared at him and pushed him away.

He shook his head and gestured futilely. She dialed back the dryer to low.

Michael watched for a moment, then looked for several seconds at Justice, what struck him most was the figure they carried away. Its face was blank.

"You are going to pay me, aren't you?" asked Frost when no one moved to give her cash.

Nin kind of snorted and turning to Wylit, pointed to a purse on the floor by *Justice*. "Give her fifteen hundred. She's done a great job! It really looks like him now."

Frost took the money with a broad smile, pleased that Nin was happy with her work, and bid everyone goodbye with a limp hand wave, and left.

Nin finally quit blowing *The Disobedient*, turned off the dryer and faced the others in the room. "Well," she began, "now we need to find Pico Eyler. He's the one who can release Wolf from this new painting. Any ideas ... besides waiting for him to track the paintings and come to us?"

"Yes," said Thena, stepping forward.

"And?"

"The Zulaika brothers must know how to reach him. He hired them after all."

"Good. Let's go visit them!" said Nin.

"Hold on," cautioned Michael. "If we all descend on them, they may just conveniently forget. So, only a few of us go. And I say rather than threaten them, we befriend them ... offer them money. They are, after all, thieves."

"Okay," agreed Nin. "But I'm going so nobody pulls a fast one."

"All right. You, Lilly, because she knows their type, and Thena because she's got access to enough money to persuade them. Fox and Tanaka can stay here with Wolf. You can go wherever you want to," he said nodding to Wylit. "And I have an errand to run," he lied. What he really wanted to do was make a phone call.

———— «◉» ————

An hour after the decision was made, Lilly, Thena, and Nin stood in the Zulaika brothers' room, waiting.

"Where do you suppose they went?" asked Lilly, addressing her question to no one in particular.

"I asked the woman on duty at the desk, who said she didn't know where specifically, but they left almost every night to play bingo for money at a private club somewhere near San Marcos. They usually wandered in angry at each other about eleven. She supposed the club shut down around ten o'clock."

"Let's hope we can bribe them," said Lilly

"I'll choke it out of them if we can't," said Nin with a disturbing gleam in her eyes.

"Better to offer them money ... enough to get their attention. They'll probably get violent if they're threatened," she offered, looking straight at Nin.

Nin sighed. "Okay. You're right. I know the type. Money talks."

"And we don't know if they got paid by Eyler since they didn't have the pictures," said Thena.

"I'm hungry," announced Lilly. "It's only nine, we've got two hours. Let's order some food."

"Or we could get drinks," said Nin.

"Why don't we just go down to the lounge, get some food and drinks, and wait. If we sit close to the door, we should hear them."

A few minutes after eleven, the women heard the stomping of feet and loud cursing in the lobby.

"You forgot the umbrella again," yelled a voice that Thena recognized as Dani.

"Yeah, well, if you hadn't wanted to play three cards at the same time, we could have won another thousand," retorted Val.

"Yeah, we could have left earlier too, before the rain."

"Jesus, does it always rain here in November?"

"Don't you swear using Jesus' name," warned Dani, "remember what Ma told us."

"Yeah, yeah, yeah."

Their voices got dimmer as they made their way down the hall to their room.

Lilly followed and waved the other two to come along. They reached the door right behind the brothers.

"Wow! Three beautiful women and the skinny blonde who stole the pictures from our storage unit," said Dani.

"We want to talk," said Lilly, pushing her way in with the Zulaikas ahead of her.

Nin and Thena followed.

The brothers stripped off their coats and tossed them on the bed by the door. Then they took off their shoes. "I'm going to take off my pants and shirt ... wet all through," Dani explained. "So, if a naked man offends you, too bad."

"Go in the bathroom," ordered Val.

Dani did, and Val threw him some dry clothes, including underwear. "So, what do you want?" he asked, directing his question at Lilly. "And," as he continued turning towards Nin, "what did you do with our pictures?"

"They weren't yours!" protested Nin, anger edging her voice. "You stole them from the old guy Marcus, and I stole them from you."

"And now, we're here to make a deal," said Thena flashing a wad of bills she pulled from her jacket pocket.

"Oh!" cooed Val softly. "We're always interested in cash. What do you in mind?"

At that time, Dani emerged from the bathroom and leered at Thena. "Would you help me zip my pants, sweetie?" he asked.

Almost before he finished the word sweetie, Nin hit him on the side of the head with the lamp and sent him reeling.

Once he caught his balance, he turned to her angrily but she had already drawn a small pistol from her pocket.

"Don't! Just don't!" she warned. "Believe me, I'd love to put one through that rat sized brain. Now, listen up! We're going to do you a favor."

"That's right," added Thena. "We know you stole the paintings for a man named Eyler."

"We want to talk to him," said Lilly. "And we figure you know how to reach him. I'm sure he left you some way to contact him, since he didn't get the pictures."

Val nodded yes. "He said if we heard from her," he nodded at Nin, "we should call him."

"So, you have a phone number," said Thena.

"Well, yeah," chimed in Dani. "But we're not telling you nothing till we hear the offer!"

Thena nodded. "Fair enough. We're proposing an exchange. We'll give you the pictures he wants plus $5,000, if you call him, tell him you got the pictures back and set up a meeting to get them to him."

"Five grand?" asked Val.

"Yes," replied Thena

"What if we just take the cash?" asked Dani.

"I shoot," said Nin. "Right through your left eye." She leveled the gun with his eye and smirked.

"Settle down Dani!" said Val, gesturing for him to stop.

Val turned to the women. "Give me a few minutes to talk to him."

They agreed and the two men disappeared into the bathroom.

The brothers emerged a few minutes later, Val smiling broadly and Dani scowling.

"Here's the deal," Val began. "We'll call him and tell him we have the pictures, but we want more money from him. That should get us a meeting. You'll give us the pictures and five thousand dollars. Once the meeting is set, only two of you can come along. You…" he pointed at Thena. "And you," he pointed at Lilly. "You," he said pointing at Nin, "can't come."

"Why not!" she protested.

"Because you're too willing to shoot us!"

"Yeah!" Dani chimed in. "I don't like that look in your eyes."

"Look," objected Nin, "I've got a king-sized interest in this. I need to go!"

"You should've been nicer," said Dani breaking into a broad smile.

"Is it a deal?" asked Val.

"Make the call," said Thena, looking at Nin in a way that said 'don't screw this up!'

Dani got the cell phone out of a gym bag in the closet and turned it on. He punched in the number for the man who hired them and listened. "Strange," he said after a few moments, "the number is disconnected."

⟢⟪⟫⟣

When he sat in the spell room as a child, he watched Solomon prepare Uriel for insertion into the art. He even kept track of the location mentally, figuring it might come in handy someday.

So, it was not much of a problem to find him once he determined that he was going to release Uriel from it.

Now, he walked casually into the Museum of Archeology in Mexico City, looking for, Chaac, the 12-foot-high Mayan god of rain with his ax raised to strike the clouds and produce lightning. He found it rather quickly since it was prominently displayed and waited until the Voladores de Papantla launched themselves from the top of a 150-foot pole and slowly descended circling it. He waited until all spectators were watching the spectacle, mumbled a spell under his breath, did a few quick hand gestures – it was the one he had best perfected -- and watched as a blue essence left the statue and coalesced into Uriel.

A few seconds later, he grabbed Uriel by the arm and steered him out of the museum.

Uriel appeared confused.

"Come on," said Crow. "I've got a car waiting."

Crow pushed him into the back seat and hopped into the driver's seat. "You look muddled," he said as he steered the Toyota Rav 4 into traffic.

"What did you expect," grumbled Uriel. "I was in that god statue for a long time."

"I understand," sympathized Crow. "But you're out now."

"Why did you get me out?"

Crow thought for an instant. "Because I think what the Sons do is cruel. So, I decided recently to go around and release as many of the fallen as I can."

Uriel was quiet after that.

They moved slowly through the heavy Mexico City traffic. No one appeared to be behind then, but Crow kept checking his rearview mirror.

After a time, Uriel noticed and asked, "Why do you keep looking in your mirrors? No one is after us. No one even saw me leave the statue. That was nicely done, by the way."

"To answer your question, someone is after me, and it's someone I don't want to meet up with."

"Oh, why is that?"

"Because if he can, he'll put me into some god forsaken piece of art for a long time."

"Oh, I see. A Son of Light."

"Yes, a very powerful one."

"Why do they do that to us?" asked Uriel after a few moments.

Crow shrugged and thought about it. "I guess it's because we're virtually impossible to kill any other way. As long as they keep refreshing the spells every hundred years or so, we're locked into the art."

"But, if they put all of us away, the world will go into entropy … the cycle of death-rebirth will be fixed forever. Remember, we only get new things from the death of the old."

Crow thought about what Uriel had said. "True. I hadn't really considered it from that point of view before."

"So, this old, powerful Son has it in for you. Why? What did you do to piss him off?"

Crow shrugged again. "If I keep moving … from captured being to captured being, it's not likely he'll catch up with me."

"But why does he have it in for you?" asked Uriel again.

"He's my mentor, so I guess he doesn't appreciate me going rogue," replied Crow finally. "And," he added after a moment, "my father was Lucifer."

Michael made his way to the breakfast room of the motel, picked a chair close to the gas fireplace, not currently lit, and thumbed the contacts icon on his phone. He punched in Graham Maxwell's home phone.

"This is Pat Maxwell. How are you Michael? We haven't heard from you in a long time. I understand that both you and Athena quit your jobs at the paper and that R.B. was furious with you."

"Hi. Nice to talk to you. I didn't know R.B. was upset. We didn't mean to cause a problem, really."

"Graham wasn't too happy either. He finds the kid who took your place too young, too uninformed, and too arrogant."

"Again, I'm sorry. Thena and I just got caught in a story we couldn't ignore."

"Oh!"

"I'll explain it in detail when we get back into town. All kinds of things have happened to us. I'll treat the two of you to a filet at Flemings and explain it. Right now, I need to talk to Graham. Is he there?"

"He's coming now. I'll give him the phone. Good to hear from you, Michael. And tell Athena I said hello."

The phone went silent for a moment. Then he heard the gravelly voice of Max.

"Michael! Haven't heard from you for quite a while. How are you?"

"Good, Max. I told Pat I'd take you and her to dinner when I got back to Cleveland, catch you both up on everything. Right now, I need a favor."

"Sure. What can I do?"

"You remember that book I gave you to store when I came back from Paris and ended up working at the paper?"

"Of course."

"I need it … and fairly quickly. Do you know where it is now?"

"Not exactly," he replied. "Remember, you seemed very intent that it be put away so neither you nor I know exactly where it was."

"Yes. You took it with you on a trip to Dallas to put together the show on Mayan art."

"Exactly. I did that. And then, I got Alfred Baker to take the book, store it, tell no one about it, and move it around every once in a while. I give him the money you send every year to keep moving it. And as far as I know, he has."

"So, right now, he's the only person who knows where it is?"

"Yep. I've never asked him about it since. I just send him the money around May 15th every year. He wanted assurance that it wasn't stolen. He's a very moral guy. So, I told him what you told me … that an older man gave it to you so it wouldn't become part of his estate when he died and become property of the State since he had no heirs."

"Good. You didn't mention that there was danger attached to it, did you?"

"No! Is there?"

"Well, I don't know exactly. Some people are now looking for it. They've become aware of it. They're thieves. Its value increases every year. The old guy who gave it to me pays me to keep it. That's the money I send you."

"Has he asked for it back?"

"No. Haven't seen him or had any other contact with him … except for the checks from a Swiss bank every year on May 1st."

"It's been twelve years … why track it down now?"

"Because I need to see exactly what's in it."

"Didn't you check it out before you gave it to me?"

"Yeah. It was beautiful, but it was in a foreign language that I didn't understand. I think it was Aramaic."

"I think you're right. I looked at it when you gave it to me and I remember seeing that it was in an ancient language. Didn't think about what it might be." He paused, "so, where do we go from here?"

"Don't know exactly, but I'd like to get hold of it and have some language expert tell me what's in it. Why don't you talk to Baker and get back to me? You've got my cell number."

"I'll call him immediately. He's still in Dallas the last I heard. I'll let you know."

CARL YOKE

Pico heard his cell phone ring and checked the identification. Not too many people knew how to reach him by phone. He answered. There was a familiar voice at the other end.

"Good to hear from you," he began.

"Likewise," Tanaka replied. She went right on. "I called to let you know that there are some people who want to talk with you about *The Disobedient.*"

"Thank you," he said. "I have been looking for that piece. I would like to see it. Where can I find them?"

"East Side Mall, two o'clock," replied Tanaka.

———— ((●)) ————

"What does he look like?" asked Fox.

"He's tall and thin with a lot of gray hair," replied Val.

"That could describe 50% of the men in this mall," said Lilly a bit exasperated.

Lilly caught Thena's eye and rolled her own eyes to express her displeasure with Val's ignorance.

Thena had been able to convince the brothers, with a small bribe, that every one of her group needed to meet Pico.

The six of them walked to a large table in the food court of the East Side Mall. Michael, Lilly and Thena sat down on one side. The two brothers and Nin sat on the other. Michael placed the large painting, wrapped in bubble wrap at the end of the table. And they waited.

"If he actually shows up, he can sit at the other end," he remarked matter-of-factly.

"And if he doesn't it's back to the drawing board," said Lilly.

After fifteen minutes Thena and Lilly went to Chipotle and brought back coffee and other drinks for the group.

As she set down the drinks she whispered to Michael, "Fox must be getting nervous. I'm sure Wolf is."

"Can he see them?" asked Michael.

"I don't think so," said Lilly. "He seems so confused."

"Here comes a man that looks like Eyler," said Thena. "I remember seeing him at an auction in Montreal."

Turning around, Dani saw him and his mouth dropped open.

"That's not him! That's not the man who hired us!"

"What are you talking about?" asked Thena.

"Just what I said. That's not the man who hired us," he protested.

"But that is Pico Eyler," she insisted.

"No," said Val. "The man who hired us was taller, sharper featured and looked like he had a constant sun tan."

Eyler approached and sat down at the foot of the table where Michael pointed.

"You all seem to be disturbed. What's going on?" asked Pico.

"There seems to be some confusion about whether or not you hired them," explained Thena.

Eyler shook his head. "Not me."

"Then who?" asked Thena.

"You say he looked like he had a sun tan?"

Dani and Val nodded.

"It can only be one person … Avanca, or Crow, as most know him."

Pico explained his relationship to Crow then sat back and surveyed the table.

"Well I do know some of you, I've been keeping tabs on you, but I don't know all of you, or exactly why you're here."

They went around the table and took turns introducing themselves.

"We brought the painting," said Michael laying a hand on the bubble wrapped painting. "We want to make a deal."

"Eh! And what's that?"

"We'll give you the painting if you'll make Wolf whole. And tell us what's going on. For example, why did the Sons of Light put me into a painting, which I didn't appreciate, by the way… and why Wolf?"

"Now wait," began Pico looking at Holland. "I had nothing to do with your confinement to the painting."

"But we saw you examining it in Montreal," Thena protested.

"Yes. That was me, but I was just trying to assess if it had been conditioned. And it had been. It had a spell on it, very deep and complex … almost as if a master like Lucifer had cast it. But, of course, it couldn't have been him because he had been dispersed by then."

"Who then?" asked Lilly.

"Well," explained Eyler, "anyone of the others like Lucifer who knew about his book of spells."

"Other fallen angels," said Thena

"Exactly, especially those who were in the poker game or were watching it when Lucifer lost his book in a reckless bet."

"Lost it?" questioned Michael.

Pico nodded.

"To whom?" asked Lilly.

"To Merlin." There was a gasp. "But he never paid up, at least not for a long time, and some of us believe that when he did it wasn't with the real book but an altered copy."

"What a rat," remarked Lilly.

Pico smiled. "He's Lucifer. What else would you expect?"

"Didn't Merlin think something was wrong?" asked Thena.

Pico sighed. "I suppose, but he had become an old fool by then, dominated by his woman, drinking and gambling."

"But still a master caster and powerful person," said Nin who had remained silent until then.

"So, you think he never had the real book?" asked Michael.

"Would you give up a book like that which could make you enormously powerful, probably the most powerful in the world."

"No," said Holland. "And I certainly wouldn't want my enemies to have it."

"Most of them are out of commission, but I've been keeping watch on the others."

"Like who?" asked Michael.

"Asmodeus, Azazel, Uriel and a few more."

"And if one of them got the book, he would be very powerful and very dangerous I presume," said Nin.

Pico nodded yes. "Remember all are full of hubris and want to control the world."

"I thought master casters didn't need a book," said Nin.

"Lucifer didn't. But these beings are not yet up to his level."

"So, if I can skip ahead, when we disposed of Lucifer, we messed up some demon's plans," said Thena.

"Yes," replied Pico. "You two made the book a mystery. Only Lucifer knew where the real book was. Now, it's all speculation."

"So, he really didn't want the Venus and the Helix?"

"Oh, he wanted them. He wanted his so-called friends to think they were important to put them off the trail."

"A red herring so to speak," said Lilly.

"Absolutely. Lucifer's very smart but subject to missing the point because he is so ego centered. And," he added "if he returns soon, he'll be after you two. He's also very vengeful."

"So, where is he now?" asked Lilly.

Pico shrugged. "I'm not sure, but I've heard beings who are dispersed end up somewhere in the seams between universes … the plasma bubbles that enclose them. It's hard to know where exactly, because there are so many universes and they bump into each other creating new ones. In the "bumping," beings sometimes get thrown through."

"So, they're disenfranchised in a sense," said Thena.

"Yes. And they may not even recall their previous existence."

"Then," began Lilly, "the various mythologies of this world come from beings bumped into it?"

"Or they were born here because their parents were bumped here. And some of those beings become unique because they gain essence from two disparate parents."

"So, it's possible that some of the tales we have actually happened," said Thena, "even as improbable as they might seem …like 'Beauty and the Beast', 'The Princess and the Frog' or mermaids."

"Yes. It's just your basic shape shifting."

There was a brief silence.

"What's the point of putting a person into a painting?" asked Michael.

"Control," replied Eyler matter-of-factly. He saw some confusion in their eyes so he continued. "It's difficult to release yourself from a painting, though sometimes it happens. And there's a fine line to tread. If the being in the painting is in darkness too long, it may cause his essence to disperse."

"So, the picture can't stay covered, or in storage indefinitely," offered Thena.

"Right. Being in a picture weakens a being, reduces its powers, and may confuse it."

"And too long in a painting that's covered may cause a person to be weakened or to disperse," said Nin.

"Right, Vivien."

Except for the Zulaika brothers, the others around the table looked startled.

"And where is Merlin? Do you still have him locked away?"

Nin's eyes widened; her jaw dropped. "How …," she gasped.

"Wyclif was Merlin," said Michael in a moment of insight.

"So was Merle," she admitted, "who told you to leave Lilly and go home."

They all sat starring, mildly stunned.

"They say confession is good for the soul," said Lilly finally and started to laugh. "But enough of it. Let's get down to business, Mr. Eyler! We want you to try to release Wolf from the picture he's in," she lied. Wolf had already been freed, but he certainly wasn't whole. "But first, tell us why you wanted the picture he was in."

"The pictures," corrected Pico. "I know he's no longer just in *The Disobedient*, and that part of his essence is in another that I've never seen."

"And why did you want them?" asked Thena.

"To try to release him, to try to make him whole, to find out how much he remembers, and to somehow protect him from powerful beings, the fallen angels, who are looking for him. And he apparently knows where the real book is."

"But why do they want the book?" asked Thena. "Don't they have powers of their own?"

Eyler nodded yes … then added, "But none were as powerful as Lucifer … their leader. He really believed he was the most powerful being in the multiverse. But that didn't make him wise."

"I see."

"Now, let's try to get Wolf out of that picture you brought. Is it *The Disobedient*?"

Michael nodded yes, stood and unwrapped the painting. Pico looked it over.

"You've already freed him, haven't you?" he said.

They all looked surprised.

"Yes," mumbled Nin, Thena, Lilly and Michael.

"Then may I see him?"

"He's not well," admitted Michael.

"We thought maybe you could 'repair'… I guess that's not the right word but … him," said Lilly.

"I'll try."

Eyler ran his hands over the painting, made several gestures, and spoke a number of words under his breath.

Nothing happened.

He tried again ... and a third time.

Then frowning he shook his head no. He sighed.

"His essence, DNA if you will, is just too messed up for this to be easy."

He was studying the paint some more when they heard yelling coming at them from the other end of the food court.

"Thena! Lilly! Wolf's been kidnapped! Help! I couldn't stop it! I tried, but I couldn't!"

Michael pulled out a seat at the table and Fox sat down hard, nearly tipping over and breathing heavily.

"What happened?" several of them asked.

We were sitting on the bench in front of Macy's. An old man came up to us with a beat-up ball cap in his hand. He was wearing a dirty New Jersey Devils hockey shirt, torn jeans and ripped shoes. He looked at Wolf and said 'Aren't you Ignatius Wolf?' in a gravel voice."

She paused and took a drink of Michael's coffee before continuing, "Wolf just looked at him blank faced. Then the man said 'you don't remember me, do you?' Wolf shook his head no. He sat down beside us, next to Wolf, and put his arm around his shoulders. 'We were at a poker game together many years ago.' Wolf seemed to brighten up. He pointed at the man, flashed a half-smile and asked 'Uriel?' The man also smiled. Then before I could even move, there was a fog in the mall ... very heavy. The next thing I saw was a huge face staring down at me. It was bald and copper skinned, with a single earring dangling from his left ear. I saw them floating away and they disappeared."

Everyone listened quietly until she finished.

"Uriel," repeated Eyler with a deep sigh. He was frowning. "This is not good ... not at all!"

The rabbit sitting nervously on the stool in the center of the circle of women sniffed furiously.

"He seems to know," whispered Raven to the women in the chair next to her.

Maria Fourbe stood in a white robe above the rabbit. "I won't hurt you," she cooed. "I'm calling you Hazel because Hazel was brave and so are you."

The rabbit turned its head and sniffed at her.

"I'll talk to you in Lapin," she cooed.

She said something softly to the rabbit that no one could hear and it's nervous sniffing immediately slowed. After a few moments, she stroked Hazel's back gently, whispered something, made some hand gestures and the rabbit dissolved into a cloud of purple smoke. Then reformed itself into a six-foot-tall Velociraptor with lavender, olive and yellow skin.

The women jumped back.

It jerked its head from side to side, flexed its taloned feet and squawked a warning at them.

Maria cooed to it, made hand gestures and spoke quietly. Amazingly it, like the rabbit, immediately quieted down, though it still flicked its tongue every few seconds.

"I will name you Rap," she said.

Then she spoke to Rap in a whisper, made more hand gestures and made another broad sweep of her arm, and Rap dissolved into a cloud of lavender mist.

More gestures, more whispering where once the stool stood, and the mist coalesced into a fifteen-foot-tall T. Rex, bent over from what was now, a too low celling that it bumped its head on.

"Easy girl," she said and quickly began the now familiar routine; cooing, gesturing, and whispering. "You are Queen!" she declared.

One last broad gesture and Queen dissolved into a multicolored mist. Another gesture and Queen became a six-foot-high Pteranodon, squawking softly from a toothless mouth and slowly moving long wings with vestigial, pale orange feathers on them.

It squawked louder when it saw her, a cry of recognition it seemed.

"Ah, Swoop," she began. "Nice to see you too." Then once again cooing, whispering, and gesturing, Swoop dissolved in a cloud of pale orange smoke and Hazel coalesced from the mist.

"It's okay girl," she said softly, picking the frightened rabbit up in her arms and stroking it's back slowly.

"I've got everything under control!"

"My God! She's gotten very good, very quickly," Raven whispered to Gina, the woman beside her.

Gina nodded, then smiled. "She seems to be a natural!"

"I know the demon who took Wolf is one of Lucifer's friends, but we've got to get him back!" said Michael.

"What can we do?" asked Fox, clearly distraught, her voice cracking.

"I have ways to track him, we'll do it right now. I need to go where this happened," Eyler said. "The longer we wait, the more difficult it will be. Will you show me?" he asked, looking directly at Fox.

"Yes," she replied. "Come this way."

She rose and waited for Eyler to follow her.

"Can we come?" Thena asked.

Fox nodded yes and led the way while Michael, Nin and Lilly fell in behind them.

Dani Zulaika announced that he and Val would stay behind and would be at Subway if someone needed them.

They threaded their way down the mall and turned in front of the Macy's entrance.

"Where were you exactly?" asked Eyler.

"There!" Fox pointed to a bench against the far wall.

Eyler examined it closely for a few moments then turned to the others. "There's a sulfur smell here. So, whoever kidnapped Wolf probably came from below recently. I can track this. Someone needs to drive."

"I'll get my car," said Nin. "It's large enough to hold all of us."

"All of you don't need to come," said Eyler.

"Oh, but we must," said the three women.

⸺◉⸺

Maria and Raven returned to her house and Raven brewed tea.

"You were magnificent tonight, my dear," said Raven.

"Thank you. I just seem to know what to do ... as if I have some kind of natural talent."

"Yes," agreed Raven. "That's it exactly. You're a natural."

The tea kettle whistled and Raven went into the kitchen.

Maria sat quietly, her hands crossed in her lap, a slight smile on her face. She was very pleased with herself. She liked these human women, even if they were too naïve to realize that for her to have learned all of that so quickly, she would have to have had other powers.

Raven came back a few minutes later with two cups of Darjeeling, cream, sugar and some pastries on a small silver tray.

"We've been talking," she began, "the other women and I, and we think you would be perfect for the coven office of Maiden. You're lovely and smart. And you've certainly learned a great deal very quickly. Would you be interested?"

Maria smiled broadly. "I would! Oh yes, I would! But tell me what I would have to do. You don't already have someone for that position?"

"No. In most covens, the Maiden office is not functional. It's just an office, of high repute, mind you, but titular. In the old days, the woman who occupied that office was supposed to be a companion to Satan, his helper, his mistress. But in modern times, those of us who simply try to be good and more or less are non-believers in formal religions … in other words, Wicca, want the person in that role to not only be attractive and smart, but also among the best at the craft."

"So, you think I'm that good?"

"Not yet," replied Raven, "but my Dear, you have unbelievable potential. We'll send you off, with your permission of course, to train with some of the best practitioners in the country, and maybe later, in the world."

Maria beamed. "I would be honored."

Raven rose, gestured for Maria to stand, and gave her a hug.

———

They found Wolf bewildered and shaking under an interstate bridge, his mouth bloody.

It had taken a half hour to find the location with Eyler leaning out the backseat window scenting the wind and complaining about the heavy sulfur smell.

Once they saw him, all of them including Nin, who had driven, got out quickly and raced to him. Fox brought a first aid kit she had found in the glove box and began to treat him.

"Who was it?" asked Pico, who was down on one knee beside Wolf.

"Frankly, I'm surprised he's still alive," said Lilly.

"Uriel," mumbled Wolf when he could get something out.

Thena gave him a bottle of water and he gulped it greedily.

"I told him," said Wolf a few moments later.

"Told him what?" asked Thena.

"Where the *Book* is… Lucifer's *Book*," then he started to laugh loudly.

"You didn't tell him the correct location, did you," asked Eyler, picking up on the laugh.

"Right! He's on a wild goose chase," Wolf replied, and began to laugh again. "I told him Lucifer had placed it in a painting. He asked which one. I refused. He hit me a few times and I pretended to give in. He smiled at me and hit me again. "Okay, okay" I told him. It's in Bosch's *The Garden of Earthly Delights*." Wolf started laughing again. "Uriel asked me where the painting was, and I told him it's in the Prado in Madrid. He can study the painting a long time before he figures out the book's not there. It's a very complex work."

"If he does figure it out, he'll come back for you," said Lilly. "I would," she added "and I wouldn't be happy."

"Not if we trick him into believing he has found the real *Book*," said Michael. "I assume he'll find nothing in the Bosch work."

Wolf nodded yes.

"Okay," Michael began, "do you know where Lucifer put the real book?"

Wolf nodded yes again.

"Then all we have to do is switch the real book with a fake one."

"So," said Pico, "one of us has to do that. We have time on our side." He turned and addressed Wolf, "now, you've got to tell us where the real book is."

Wolf sighed. "I've held that secret for so long I'm reluctant to tell anyone. It's like a special friend."

They all stared at him in anticipation.

"Okay," he said grudgingly, "it's in a picture by Francisco Goya, entitled The Mad Carnival, virtually unknown to the art world. It was looted from a Polish Jewish family, secured by Hermann Goring for the art collection at Linz, Austria, and disappeared after WWII. It's suspected that the picture, now worth several hundred thousand dollars, accompanied a former Nazi scientist and his wife, daughter, and son down through Italy, with the help of an element in the Catholic church to a ship that took them to Rabat, Morocco. From there they traveled to Panama and then to Puerto Rico. The church helped him escape from Germany because his wife was Catholic and he had been forced to work for the Third Rich by the Nazi's threatening to kill her and their two small children."

"So, you're saying that the picture hangs in that family's house?" said Nin.

Wolf nodded yes.

Michael spoke up, "It's really a long story but I have Merlin's copy of the *Book*. Lilly and Thena have heard the story entirely but I'll make it short. I met Merel or Merlin in Paris and he gave me the book for safe keeping. I didn't know what it was at the time but it can help us now. We can use it to trick Uriel."

"So," began Thena, "we need to get Merlin's copy of the book, go to Puerto Rico, gain entry to the house of the family that has the painting..."

"Now Perez," interrupted Wolf, "they changed their family name when they arrived in Panama."

"...and enter its world, find the real *Book*, and replace it before Uriel catches up with us."

"Yes," agreed Pico.

"Sounds like a job for Superman," joked Thena.

"Or the Mission Impossible crew" added Lilly.

"So, how do we proceed?" asked Nin.

Michael turned to Thena. "Baby, since you and Lilly know where the copy is, why don't you two go get it."

She nodded okay.

He then turned to Nin. "If you will, rent us a plane that can be ready to go to Puerto Rico early tomorrow."

"What will you do?" asked Nin.

"I'll get book covers made" said Michael.

"Red leather embossed with a silver satyr head on it?" asked Pico.

"Exactly! Deception and distraction" replied Michael.

"And what should I do?" asked Pico.

"Figure out how we can let Uriel know he's in the wrong place without letting him know that we're setting him up."

"And when we get to the Perez house, I'll take the fake book into the picture and retrieve the real one."

"Not a good idea," said Thena. "Too obvious. I think Lilly or I should take it."

"I'm going too," added Nin.

Thena shrugged. "Okay."

"I can get Merlin to help," she said.

Pico shook his head no. "He's too much of a loose cannon," he said. "But we can use him later, so keep track of him."

"Well," Nin agreed. "That's true."

"We need Uriel to think he's got the right book," said Michael "and we need for him to not take anything out on Wolf."

❧

"We have a plan then," said Pico. "Any questions or concerns?"

"I think Fox should take Wolf away from here. Someplace where it would be difficult for Uriel to find him," said Thena. "Try not to leave an obvious trail. No cell phone contact, no credit cards. Buy a burner phone. Call me with the number and I'll let you know when we succeed at this."

"Okay. I have a place in mind."

"The rest of you, keep your phones on and close," she added

"Let's get to it!" said Lilly.

"Everyone who is going, meet at the airport tomorrow morning," said Pico.

━━━━━⊰⬥⊱━━━━━

It had been snowing lightly and a few flakes still floated down as they sat in Raven's 2010 silver Audi, in the parking lot of Lake Park. It was mid-afternoon and they had come from a regional spell-casting conference in Ft. Collins. They were both sipping coffee they'd gotten at Starbuck's on their way. In front of them was a sidewalk, then a short wall and then Marshall Lake. Snow melt had puddled on the sidewalk in front of them.

"You've grown remarkably fast," said Raven. "I've never seen anything like it."

"Thank you, Tilly. I appreciate your help."

"It's my pleasure. Show me what you've learned so far," said Raven with a broad smile. She pointed to a woman in a brown coat wearing high heels and walking a golden cocker spaniel on a purple leash. "See what you can do with them!"

Maria leaned forward and studied the pair for a few seconds. Then she whispered a spell and made several gestures with her left hand.

A blue haze appeared around them, bubbled, and reformed. It became a female Neanderthal walking a small velociraptor about the size of a bird dog on a leash.

Raven burst into laughter. "Very nice," she giggled. "You know, of course, that they didn't' exist at the same time."

"Of course! But I wanted to show you what I can do."

"And you have," she replied very serious. "For a young person, you're not only a quick study with oodles of talent, you've got imagination and a sense of humor. I see great success in your future."

They landed at the Luis Munoz Marin International Airport and rented a car. There were five of them: Holland, Thena, Nin, Pico and Lilly. Nin had recruited Merlin to protect Fox and Wolf, though it was understood that if Uriel found them, they should let him believe that he was forcing information from them. They would tell him where the *Book of the Horned God* was so he could follow them into the picture.

Meanwhile Thena and Lilly had retrieved the copy from the storage unit where Baker had last left it over a year ago and it was now in Thena's possession. They had wrapped it carefully to protect it and Thena carried it in a reinforced backpack.

It took almost an hour to get the rental car, load everyone in, clear the airport and head for Punta Santiago where Cristo Perez had a house looking out on to the Pasaje de Vieques. Cristo was a business man who was in New York City with his family, having received a phone call informing him that he had won an all-expenses paid vacation for the whole family. Arrangements Lilly had handled before they left.

So, the house was unoccupied when the black Mercedes pulled into Cristo's driveway.

They stood in the living room gazing at the very large painting. Goya's *Mad Carnival* was filled with colorful figures reminiscent of the *commedia dell'arte.* The ocean lashed at the beach outside the 50's style picture window and a patio ran between the palms.

Pico sighed, and sized up the group. "Are all of you ready?" he asked. They nodded as one.

"Okay. Here we go," he said with another sigh.

He made several, subtle but complex hand motions, and each of them heard a whoosh, felt cold air rush by, saw nothing but fog and fell forward.

Thena felt cold, an icy wind, and then she tumbled into the world of the painting. She rose to one knee. No one else was with her; no Michael, Pico, Nin, or Lilly.

Instead, to her right, down the strawed pathway in front of several concession stands selling food and presenting games of chance, two tall, masked people, she assumed to be men, watched her. She stood, and one of them, the one with an olive-green clown mask came over to her and grabbed her left elbow.

"Thou art a beauty," he said in archaic English.

"Pantalone and I saw you tumble into our carnival. From whence do you come?"

"I come from the other side of the fog," she replied as she fumbled for an answer that would make sense to him. "And why are you speaking such archaic English?"

"Other side of the fog?" questioned Pantaloon, ignoring her question. "I didn't' know there was anything on the other side of the fog," he said, as he tried to grasp the meaning of her comment.

"I am Bassoon," said the tall, skinny man at her arm. "Come over here," he pointed to a tent several yards away behind a stand that read 'waffle ears' and steered her towards the opening in the tent with a large hand on her left buttock.

She smacked it away and glared at him.

"What have thee in thy satchel, little lady?" asked Pantalone, who walked ahead of the other two.

She ignored him.

"I say my lovely; what have you on your back?" he asked again, more menacingly.

"Something I have to deliver," she snapped.

He chuckled. She couldn't see his face, but the slight laugh was sarcastic.

"He said someone would come sooner or later," said Bassoon.

"We hath been waiting a long while," added Pantalone. "But he who comes was to be seeking the master's property, not delivering."

A short being with a tiny, pointed head, duck walked by, smiling. "Hi boys," she said.

"Hi, Reesie," they said as one.

"Cummin' to da' show?" Reesie asked.

"Maybe later," Bassoon replied.

"I be doin' a strip," Reesie said with a broad smile and a flutter of her eyelashes. "Who dat?" asked Reesie as she waddled by.

"Just someone we picked up," said Pantalone and they both smiled as if they shared a secret.

"Best feed dem before youse use dem up," cautioned Reesie. "Dey last longer dat way." She winked and then moved on.

Pantalone stopped in his tracks frowned, and then turned to Bassoon. "I think the lass is right," he said.

Bassoon grabbed Thena's right wrist and pulled her to the nearest stand. She winced as she neared it. There was a distinct smell of sulfur the closer they got.

When they reached it, a heavy man with bumps all over his face and arms, sidled up and ladled a scoop of pea green, soupy gelatin onto a ceramic plate and handed it to Bassoon. He then handed it to Thena with a plastic spoon and he urged her to eat.

She forced back a gag, took it, and after the bumpy man handed plates of the same stuff to Bassoon and Pantalone, she pretended to eat some but really dumped it into the bushes along their path.

She knew that resisting them would be hopeless. But as she slowly made her way towards the red and white waffle ears tent a few yards away, she noticed that there were rides further down the midway. One in particular caught her attention – what appeared to be an entrance like a tunnel of love. But the entrance was shaped like a mouth with grotesquely painted bright red lips.

She decided she would make her way there at the first opportunity.

Pantalone grabbed her arm as they approached what looked to be another woman and steered her to the side. The woman was taller than either of them, very thin and wasp-waisted. Her eyes glowed red and her very long, thin tongue was flanked by rows of small, sharp teeth.

"Boys," she began when she was close enough. "What do you have there?" She stared at Thena. "A tasty morsel?" she asked as her eyes widened and her tongue flicked.

They ignored her. "Keep moving," urged Pantalone.

"What would you take in trade?" the woman asked.

"Sorry Gormah," said Bassoon, "not available."

"Oh," Gormah cooed, "come on baby. Surely there is something."

"No," replied Bassoon. "We're keeping this one. She tumbled in from the fog. Look at that body. She can amuse us for days before we use her up."

"Might I have her then?" asked Gormah.

"Perhaps," he answered, then smiled and pushed Thena ahead of himself. "Keep moving," he whispered.

A large leather winged bird glided over them. It's only sound was the occasional flap of its large wings.

With a slight squawk, the bird suddenly dived down and grabbed Gormah in its talons. Its flapping to lift her from the ground caused Pantalone and Bassoon to scramble to get out of the way and Thena pulled free.

She ran immediately for the entrance to the tunnel she had

seen earlier, past other noisy rides, stands of unusual looking and smelling food, and passed many odd creatures – the type of being's nightmares are made of.

She reached the entrance to the ride before Pantalone or Bassoon could recover, noting that painted on the tunnel marquee above the entrance were the words "River Styx."

Boats were plying a water course, mostly empty, moving swiftly in the rapid stream. She leaped into the one nearest her, landed feet first, and then fell heavily to her knees. She noticed blood on her right kneecap. For the next few seconds, she dabbed at the bloody kneecap with a tissue she found in her pocket and settled back against the molded plastic seat.

The boat bumped from side to side as its channel twisted, turned and steadily descended. Around each bend where scenes of death or Hell. She wondered about the scenes from Hell, since it was strictly a Christian idea, and it dawned on her that Lucifer had been one of the Christian fallens.

As the boat twisted, turned and banged against the rock that shaped its course, her mind played with several ideas.

Hell was Christian, so was the river Styx and Lucifer wasn't the horned, hoofed, pointed tailed being of popular myth with red skin, a pitchfork, and glowing eyes. Indeed, that was a relatively new evolution in the history of the religion derived from the satyr of Greek myth. And the fallen beings were cast into Tartarus, not Hell according to John Milton's *Paradise Lost*.

So, she reasoned, Lucifer's "bread crumbs" were likely within Christianity, probably in *The King James Bible*. That made sense to her.

She had been seeing the numbers on some of the walls as the boat descended, but she could only remember one. Was that a clue from Genesis? The only direction she could remember in that book was east of Eden. Had she gone east after she tumbled into the picture world? She had no way to reference her direction. But if the

Styx tunnel led to another clue, then she must have gone East for her hypothesis to make sense.

Suddenly she remembered Pico talking about Wolf's memory problems. He said that prolonged habitation in a "picture world" often disturbed, or even changed thinking, especially memory. He didn't know if the damage was permanent, but the longer the habitation, the more likely it was to be.

So, maybe her reasoning was sound and Lucifer did leave himself clues to the location of his *Book*. And maybe the clues were somehow connected to the Christian Bible. She'd done her bachelor's degree at Ohio Wesleyan University, so she had taken a semester in the Old Testament. Then because she came to view all religion as different interpretations of the same basic ideas, those that evolved as attempts to explain that which is common to all beings and ultimately unknowable, she took more religion. Or to put it more succinctly, mythology. Including the *New Testament*. None of it made literal sense, but it didn't have to, to serve its purpose.

Well, she would perhaps have an answer to her hypothesis at the next turn or descent … for she had been steadily dropping.

She leaned back, closed her eyes, and let the tunnel take her away.

Fox had rented a luxury condo in Estes Park. It was a mile from the entrance to Rocky Mountain National Park and three miles from the heart of town. She had registered under the name of Eleanor Rigby. Wolf was Laurence Talbot. It seemed appropriate since Talbot was also confused in many ways.

Merlin arrived the morning of their second day and settled into the empty bedroom, still in his 'buff' young man form. He admitted he liked it because women were falling all over themselves to please him.

There was a deck overlooking Fall River, which wound through a stand of pines. Fox and Wolf had gone out briefly but it was cold and began to snow. So, they came back in, made a pot of coffee, and curled up in front of the fireplace.

It all seemed tranquil especially since the snow picked up that evening. The three of them got to know each other and discussed the problem.

They were surprised when there was a knock at the door about noon the next day. Merlin was closest so he went to open it. When he did, a tall, bald man smiled at him. "I'm looking for Ignatius Wolf," he began. Then without waiting for a response, he said, "you must be Merlin, sent to protect him, no doubt," and still smiling raised his right arm and fired a bolt of energy at him.

Merlin dissolved in a flash of blue light before the others even knew what happened. Then Uriel looked from side to side and in a mocking gesture, blew on the tip of his pointer finger as if he'd fired a gun. He noticed Fox and Wolf sitting by the fireplace and swelled up until his head nearly touched the celling of the condo. He looked like a float in the Macy's Thanksgiving Day parade as he glided over to where they sat.

He smiled down at Wolf.

"You need to tell me now," he boomed, "where is Lucifer's *Book*?"

"And if I don't?" replied Wolf. "You can't kill me."

"I know. You are to tarry until He returns. But, while I may not be able to kill you," a wicked smile spreading across his face, "I can make your life miserable."

"I've been imprisoned. You can't hurt me anymore!"

Uriel considered Wolf's statement and after a few moments shapeshifted to normal human size.

"I suppose you're right," he admitted. Then he nodded toward Fox, "But I can hurt her."

Wolf's face went pale. He looked at Fox and then stared at the floor for almost a minute.

"Okay," he said finally. "Okay. The *Book* is in an oil painting entitled *Mad Carnival* by Francisco Goya."

"Thank you. Where is it?"

"Puerto Rico," Wolf answered, then after a thought asked, "by the way, how did you know that the *Book* wasn't in the Bosch?"

Uriel shrugged. "Simple. The *Book* has its own microbiome. I didn't detect it at any time I was in *The Garden of Delight*. All I found there was noise and chaos. So, I came looking for you."

Uriel turned to leave but paused after a few steps and looked back over his shoulder at Wolf, "Need I tell you to stay out of this?" He shifted his eyes to Fox, "I will kill her if you interfere."

Wolf nodded that he understood.

⸺ ✹ ⸺

The trip down the water chute was brutal – swift, bumpy, and dangerous. But eventually it opened out onto a broad lake in an enormous cave. Her boat lost momentum as it distanced itself from the end of the chute. Thena could see large, calcified formations, some like icicles, high above her. Many of them were reddish, and she presumed that part of their color came from iron ore embedded in them. Looking closely at the water below the boat, she saw that it too, on close examination, was tinted slightly reddish.

She was also aware of a smell, a mixture of sulfur and something else … like decomposing flesh and death.

There were things in the water. She could not see them, but she could hear them. They were murmuring something that was not quite understandable. It sounded to Thena like "she's the one. But she doesn't know it." Then she felt the boat rock from waves. Something was rising below it. The smell of decomposing flesh grew stronger and the water glowed red like it was on fire. Directly in front of her appeared a huge head. She threw her arms across her face to block the smell, which was overpowering and blinked to clear the stinging tears that the smell produced.

The head was enormous and looked dragonish, with marbled skin in different shades of red, pink and purple. The mouth was large and contained a double row of razor-sharp teeth with a long, forked tongue. Its eyes were golden.

"We don't see many like you here," it began. "Almost all are human."

The importance of the beast's words were lost on Thena and she could only stare.

It snorted, like a chuckle.

"What brings you to the Master's realm?" it asked.

"Who are you?" she countered.

The beast snorted again. "I am Kerbus," it answered. "Again, I wonder, why are you here? You are not a dead human, so what business have you here?"

Thena hesitated for just an instant. Then answered "I came bearing a gift for him."

"You know, no one can just enter his kingdom."

"Of course. But … here let me show you." She reached into the pocket of her jeans and pulled out her cell phone. She thumbed it open, found the icon for recorded music, quickly toggled down to Smetana's *Moldau* and pressed it.

The music began slowly … a rolling, lilting musical metaphor for the source of the river. Kerbus listened intently, Thena watched. Kerbus' eyelids drooped. The music moved faster. The beasts' eye's closed. Thena held her breath. Kerbus snored softly. Thena laid the phone on the seat, took oars from the bed of the boat, put each in an oarlock and began to row slowly.

Lilly landed feet first in rain and mud, staggered forward and fell on her face. She was in an area bare of vegetation, except for brown, dead grass, mostly mashed flat and small trees stripped bare of bark in most places. The tree branches were black and thorny.

She made it to her feet and stumbled forward. Then she stopped. She had no idea which way she should go. Her main purposes were to mislead any pursuers and fight them if she got the chance. While she had no special powers like some of the others, she had stashed a short sword in her jacket and a .45 caliber pistol in her pocket.

It dawned on her that she was woefully unprepared to battle any of the fallen. She, and the others, all thought they would end up in the same place. Then, perhaps one of the others, Pico, Michael or Nin, would dispatch Uriel and she would not have to deal with him.

Maybe she should just find cover and "hunker down," metaphorically speaking, until something resolved itself. But how would she know. Her cell phone had no bars.

She slugged forward, figuring that if anyone was looking for her, moving made her less of a target. The rain beat at her, the wind howled, and her eyebrows iced up. Then she heard another sound, lower than the wind, that chilled her. She hurried forward, slipping in the wet mud, then falling, rising and moving on as fast as she could.

The sound, a deeper, longer howl, was closer and moving faster than she could. She found a dead limb on a tree in front of her and broke it off to use as a walking stick. It helped as she slipped and trudged forward.

The thing howled again and fear rose in her throat.

Lilly stumbled, fell, rose, stumbled, rose and tried to run. She breached a hill, slipped, fell forward, and tumbled down a steep slope, banging into dead bushes, hearing them snap. Then falling through snow and rain, down, down, down into darkness.

She landed in a rapidly moving river of icy water that plunged into a cave. She was falling again.

When she finally landed, she was in water up to her waist. Above her, the thing that was following her peered down at her and snarled.

She sighed, pulled out the .45, cocked it, and fired. The wolfish thing tumbled into the water, splashed a few times and was quiet.

"Well," she breathed, "at least one of them won't be following."

———— ◆ ————

Nin was angry when she landed feet first in a small clearing. She didn't expect to be by herself. She had learned a lot from Merlin, but she wasn't sure it was enough to face a creature as powerful as Uriel alone.

Giant trees as big as sequoias blocked the light. She could not identify them but their trunks were perhaps twenty feet in circumference and their branches intermingled to create the effect of a dome. She was stunned when a bolt of what looked to be lightening crashed into the top of one of the giants without warning. The blast showered sparks around her and the tree top blazed, creating light in the canopy and filling her eyes with acid smoke, making them burn and water.

She moved to an alley of trunks to her right, away from the fire and smoke. She came to a second clearing and almost upon her arrival another bolt struck a few yards behind her. That burst set underbrush burning and she moved on down the pathway.

Then she heard muted laughter and talking from the treetops.

Another burst, smaller, hit behind her.

Then she heard more talking.

"Faster, faster," came one voice. "To the pit."

"What's the hurry?" came second voice on the other side of the path. "It's fun to play with the trespassers."

"The Master wouldn't like it," said the first, clearly concerned.

"Well, all right," replied the second reluctantly.

Another bolt broke close on her heels and she jumped and hurried along.

She heard the heavy flap-flap of wings, stopped and turned, and tried to glimpse what was following above. But all she saw where very large shadows, bat-shaped.

Two flashes erupted behind her and she ran ahead of the flaming brush and smoke.

In a few minutes, she broke from the trees at the edge of the forest and urged on by shaft after shaft of lightning, she ran faster.

She didn't see the pit in the ground. She fell over it, pitched forward, and fell several feet into wet earth face down.

As she rolled on to her back, the pit filled with flashes of lightning, so bright she could not make out the sky.

She hunkered down as light flashed all around her and tried to figure out what to do next.

———⟨●⟩———

When Michael tumbled into Goya's *Mad Carnival*, he found himself trying to maintain his balance on the side of a volcano spewing ash from its core and threads of lava flowing from a fissure just under its top. The ground was hot and he could feel rumbling every few moments through his boots. They had all chosen boots for just such an instance.

Several hundred feet above him two narrow rivers of lava oozed slowly closer. They crackled and crunched, almost as if they were speaking.

He watched as the two streams merged and it began to hiss. Ash filled the sky and he found breathing difficult. He edged down the slope away from the advancing lava stream which seemed to be growing wider with every second. He spent a few moments studying the volcano, first to his left and then to his right. There seemed to be no route for escape.

As the lava, which was flowing very slow, neared, he was certain he heard it speaking, in at least two voices.

"The Master ordered us to not let anyone pass," said the first, high-pitched and feminine. "We must do what he commands," she continued.

"And we shall," replied the second, "but we are only one of several traps he set on the way to Lake Cocytus. So even if we fail, others will help us."

"We will look better in his eyes if we succeed," said the female.

"Then let's hurry," said the second voice, "he can't go anywhere. We can burn him up."

"Yes," agreed the female. "Let's join the others and create a river."

Michael listened carefully. So, there were other traps.

The voices were right, there was nowhere to go but down, and so he did … slowly.

At some point, a few minutes later, the joined streams of lava, their tops black from cooling, split into wider rivers and flowed to either side of him as if they wanted to prevent him moving east or west.

"Why would they do that?" he wondered. It occurred to him that perhaps they did not know if he had some special powers. After all, they did not know him.

But he had none, so he kept slowly descending. His purpose was to protect Thena and Lilly.

After several minutes punctuated by tremors and hiccups of ash, he reached the edge of a cliff.

He could see water below and dark circles of blue where it was deeper. So, this volcano rose right from the floor of the sea.

It was very hot. He was sweating. Twilight was gathering. He had no place to go.

———⊶⊙⊷———

Thena left the boat on the bank of the Styx and stepped on to the shore. It was muddy and there were puddles in what she quickly determined were footprints. She tried to avoid stepping in them because if she did, she might sink into some mire.

And there were things in the puddles, squishy wiggly things that seemed to murmur endlessly. She could not make out what they were saying.

The only light came from the glow of a city quite a way off. It was walled she could see, but the tops of a number of structures showed black against the fiery red background behind them.

She slogged on towards the city. Perhaps she thought someone there could direct her to the location of the *Book*. Then it occurred to her that since she was to take the real book and replace it with the one she carried, maybe asking for directions was not a good idea. If Uriel came this way, which seemed likely, someone might mention her interest in the *Book* to him or one of the others who might be seeking it. On the other hand, the fallen were so incredibly self-centered and proud, they probably wouldn't take the threat of a human looking for the *Book* seriously.

She trekked on, past odd shaped rock formations alive with small snarling, furry creatures that resembled meerkats and seemed fully bent on killing her. But as mean as they sounded, they never ventured more than a few yards toward her, apparently afraid to leave a short retreat to safety in case she turned out to be dangerous.

Large bats swooped down at her from some unseen perch, but they too veered away when they got close. And a brigade of what appeared to be small, dinosaurs ... or maybe some kind of lizard that walked on two legs ... stopped momentarily in front of her, chattered at her, ran towards her, splashing water, blood, and mud as they did, then retreated. It reminded her of someone challenging her. But a few of her dance moves and they backed away into the darkness. They were perhaps just trying to get a feel for the level of threat she posed.

She trudged on towards the city. As she drew closer, she could see that much of the wall ahead was in ruin.

Then, out of smoke that rose from fissures in front of the main gate, a massive gothic arch, something appeared.

It was twice her size, horned and dark skinned with gray splotches and yellow feathers down its spine.

"I smell you," it began. It sniffed the air, "you smell like a woman. You would be quite tasty roasted over a fire!"

"I need to pass" countered Thena. "I am a messenger, carrying something for Lucifer."

The creature snarled something that sounded like a laugh.

"I doubt it," said the creature. "We haven't seen the Master in ages and he directed us to stop any intruders from passing through here – demon, monster, angel or whore. You look like a jezebel to me and I will have my way with you before I kill you."

Thena was stymied. She didn't relish a battle with this creature. It would probably kill her and then the entire mission would be over.

"She is none of those, Krat. Now back off! That's an order!" came a voice from behind her. "You do not know who you are messing with."

"I am the Mayor of Dis and I intend to carry out the Master's orders," roared the creature as he gestured to the city behind him.

"She has great powers of her own, but even if she did not, I am here to see that she gets safe passage. You may well be the Mayor of Dis, but I am Queen of this realm and she is under my protection."

Krat glared defiantly, then snarled, his long-forked tongue darting in and out rapidly in anger.

"Let her go down through the tunnels under the city," he snarled.

"No!" said the person behind Thena. "It will not be!"

A shaft of lightning, screamed by Thena and dug into the ground a few inches in front of Krat.

He jumped back, startled and stumbled to the side.

"All right, all right," he conceded. "But," he began again, "you keep her on the road to the south gate. No detours. No sightseeing. No interfering with the work inside. You guide her through. No more."

The person behind Thena, considered Krat's rules with several loud "humm's" and then agreed.

Thena felt a hand on her shoulder, gently pushing her forward. It was delicate, pale and long-fingered. She could see out of the corner of her eye.

"Come, dear. Follow me!" And the person behind Thena, a woman in a tight black dress pushed by her.

"Who are you?" asked Thena as the woman passed.

"I am Queen of the Underworld," the woman said. Then, in a whisper, "Persephone."

Thena fell in behind Persephone and in a few moments, they passed under the massive onyx arch. There was a fetid smell just inside the gate and pools of decaying vegetation for several yards on both sides of a mud path running with what appeared to be blood.

Ahead, Thena could see more pools and a demon, a miniature, lizard-like creature pushing several humans down into a pit of sewage, cackling the whole time.

She shuddered as they moved on through the city. Both left and right were tortures of various kinds: iron maiden, bed of Procrustes, a jousting dummy, and quartering by small, dinosaur creatures. The ground ran in rivers of blood, the air was heavy with sulfur, and periodically she would hear sexual comments from the Satyr-like creatures: "I'm horny," "I'll screw you to death," "My organ plays a merry tune. You'll sing to it." But they dared not approach her. Persephone shoved them away with a wave of her hand and a warning to keep their distance.

They walked on, Thena careful to stay only a few steps behind Persephone. Though she could not see a specific path, Persephone seemed to be following one. There were only a few turns; most of the structures were in ruin, but coming from them were sobs, screams, cries for mercy, the crash of whips, moans, and promises, rephrased several different ways to be good if only given another chance.

Thena caught the scream of what seemed to be a child and turned as if to go to it, but Persephone grabbed her by the left elbow and stopped her.

She was smiling slightly. "It is not what it seems," she said. "And you must not leave the path of my protection."

Thena gave her a questioning look and Persephone continued. "Regardless of your powers and who you are, they will rape you, then kill you, and cut you into bits. But unlike the others who are tortured here, you will not be restored."

Thena nodded.

"You do understand, correct?"

"Yes. But I've got a lot of questions."

"I'm sure you do," said Persephone as she stopped on the path, turned to face Thena, and pushed back her cowl.

Thena stared for a moment. Persephone was beautiful. In the light from the city, Thena saw mid length auburn hair, a heart shaped face, and almond eyes with no irises – only pupils.

"How lovely you are," complimented Thena.

"Thank you my dear. One gets few compliments down here. Most of the male figures, and some of the females, are simply salacious."

"Why are you helping me?" asked Thena.

"Because you are on a journey of self-discovery and self-fulfillment. It's a journey I have made many times myself. And no one, even if dead, can make this trip by herself. Helping is what I do."

"Thank you," said Thena. "Can you also tell me why, when I first got near the city, the creatures, like the little lizards didn't attack me?"

"Come," started Persephone, "let's walk while we talk. I'd like to get you out of here as soon as possible. It'll minimize possible danger to you. There are a few perils here that even I cannot protect you against." They moved on side by side, "Now as to why those creatures did not continue their attack. Well dear, you have powers of some nature. You may not be aware of them, but you have inherited some. The creatures fear what they may be."

"I do?" said Thena, puzzled. "I'm not aware of any powers in my family."

Persephone shrugged. "Perhaps not, but I can read your biome, and I assure you, you are not like other humans, you are gifted."

The road turned along a river and Thena could see bodies floating along, face up, their expressions twisted in anguish and their mouths moving. Saying something she couldn't make out.

"Who are they?" she asked as she shied away from the bank.

"That is the River of Lost Souls. Those who float by committed suicide. They won't hurt you unless you actually get into the river. I don't suggest it however, that is blood they float in, not water."

"Is this one of several underworlds ... I mean, you are a Greek Goddess but this looks like it is Christian, a variation of Dante's *Inferno*."

Persephone smiled at her. "There is only one underworld and one Queen. What you see is colored by the culture you grew up in, and I go by many names."

Persephone pointed ahead to a ruined brick building, "We have to go through there to get to the passage which will take you to the Taenarus Cave and then to the surface. But remember the surface I mention is inside the Goya painting, not your world."

Thena nodded.

"Come," said Persephone. "The only way to get to the passage and out of the city goes through this building, The House of Ghosts."

Thena followed Persephone through a broken walled opening into a dark tunnel that, after a few minutes, opened into a large room.

"Be careful not to get too close to the glass in the walls. The powers there will suck you into yet another world from which there is no escape that I know of. I've been told the only exit is the same as the entrance."

"Who are those people with their hands pressed against the glass with despair on their faces?" asked Thena.

"Ah," Persephone answered, "those are the vain."

Thena nodded that she heard but said nothing. Two ideas struck her almost simultaneously. She knew how to get rid of Uriel, and she knew how to find the real *Book*.

***

Michael closed his legs and drew in his arms. Hitting the water from the height he was could hurt a person badly if he didn't make himself as compact as possible. He also had to be sure he went in feet first. If his legs were spread or he suddenly twisted to the side, his arms were out, or his head was up, he could hurt himself badly.

He'd learned all that in Navy flight training. What one wanted to avoid at all costs was losing consciousness. Then a person could not save himself, he would have to rely on a life jacket or another person. Neither of which was an option.

Not only that, he wasn't dressed for a swim. His jackets and boots were too heavy.

But he hit the water perfectly.

Once under, he pushed both arms out level with his shoulders;

which quickly slowed his descent. He had filled his lungs just before he hit the water so he knew he could stay down for a bit, but after a few moments he bobbed to the top.

The question now was what to do next. He needed to move away from the lava now pouring into the sea since it now had awakened and even though slow moving, would do all it could to stop him.

He looked around. The volcano took up most of the island where he had landed, but ahead were three islets at varying distances, and farther on were others. By their diminishing size and color, he determined they were a chain. None it appeared were erupting, so he lowered his head and began to swim to the nearest one.

⸎

When Pico landed, he found himself on the back of a white dragon.

"It'll be a pleasure to eliminate you," said Uriel raising himself to twelve feet high and blowing fire from his nose in a steady stream.

Pico stared at him, shoved his feet deeper into the stirrups, and steadied the dragon by patting its neck with his right hand and talking to it lowly.

"You've been a pain in our collective necks for too long. My peers will thank me for getting rid of you."

Uriel had shifted to a bald headed, well-muscled man with dark, deep set eyes and an earring in his left ear.

"You need to go back to where you came from," said Pico.

"I will do what I want," said Uriel.

The wind howled, and falling hail turned into a furious flurry of snow.

Pico started, "You learned nothing during your imprisonment!

You're still so arrogant that you believe no one can stop you! It's that arrogance which will allow The Sons of Light to succeed."

Uriel laughed mockingly. "When I have Lucifer's *Book* then no one will stand in my way."

"Dream on," said Pico confidently. "There are a whole battery of people here in this picture, who will go to unforeseen lengths to be sure that never happens. One of them will succeed."

"Nonsense," said Uriel. "Lucifer left many traps. And though I don't know where the *Book* is, I can read the "microbiome" of its leather and like a good bloodhound I'll just follow its trail until I find it. Just like I followed yours to find you."

Pico sighed deeply. He was in no mood for Uriel's games.

"And what is this puffery with dragons, and lances, and fire."

Uriel laughed, deep and loud. Then he shrugged.

"A moment of inspiration." He smiled broadly. "A medieval duel, right out of *Ivanhoe*."

"The snow," which was now falling heavily, "will make the fire sticks virtually useless," he said.

"Snow, fire, fierce wind … none of it matters. When I dispose of you, all you meddling Sons of Light will know my power."

"So," said Pico, "this is a show."

"Of course, a morality play." He laughed. "Perhaps I should instead characterize it as a negative morality play."

Uriel suddenly slapped his black-skinned dragon on the flank with his right hand. The beast lunged forward, sent lasers of flame from its nostrils, and Uriel lowered his lance as if he were going to charge.

Pico backed away. His white dragon was nearly invisible in the increasingly heavy snow.

Then Uriel stopped, laughed, and moved slowly forward, smoke leaking from his dragon's nose flaps.

Pico instructed his dragon, Nimbus, to back up another step. He wanted a better angle. Then, he reasoned, he would charge.

But he suddenly felt the hind quarters of his ride sliding slowly down a grade. In a few moments Nimbus was breaking through ice and they were both sinking.

Uriel stood over them blocking Nimbus' attempt to pull them out of the water.

Pico cast a bolt of lightning at Uriel only to have it blocked when Uriel produced a shield. The bolt deflected harmlessly away into the storm.

Nimbus sank farther. Icy water was up over his saddle.

Pico cast a heavy chain at a nearby oak tree. It wrapped around the trunk and anchored itself in the crotch of two thick limbs.

But Uriel, his face a frozen smile, shot an energy beam at the chain, that quickly melted it through. And Pico felt himself, still on the back of his dragon, sinking into the water ... waist deep, then shoulder deep, and finally neck deep. Nimbus struggled to pull them out, but there was no bank to cling to and he sank. He let out a soft squeal.

Pico also continued to sink.

Uriel, now off his dragon, stood over them clapping wildly.

Pico submerged. Nimbus sank deeper and deeper. Pico could barely see him. He was just a shadow.

Then Uriel was waving his arms in what seemed to be an animated and swift fashion and the water above Pico's head turned dark and began to thicken.

He struggled upward, pushed against it when he reached it and cursed. It was solid.

He tried several quick spells, but nothing. Then exhausted he sank deeper.

They left the House of Ghosts and followed the path by the river, Persephone on the bank side and Thena on the inside.

"Do any of the fallen come here?" asked Thena.

"Rarely," replied Persephone with a slight smile. "They have no reason to come here, and they're all about reason."

Then she turned to Thena, her face questioning.

"It didn't occur to ask you this before, but why are you here? Humans don't come here without cause only if they are dead."

Thena considered her answer carefully. "I'm on a mission," she said finally, "to deliver a package."

"Is it important?" asked Persephone.

Thena nodded and added, "Very."

Persephone nodded in return. "I see."

"Don't you want to know what it is?"

"No. It's none of my business. My job is guide. You are making a trip of self-fulfillment. To help you succeed is my only concern. In effect I help your old life end and give you a new one. When you leave here, you will be a new person with new characteristics and attitudes."

Thena was puzzled but said nothing. What did Persephone mean?

They followed the river which bent back to the right around yet another building ruin. Then Persephone suddenly stopped and grabbed Thena's shoulder to hold her back.

"What is it?" asked Thena.

Persephone pointed. "There along the bank ... the figure in white. We must approach her cautiously. She is very dangerous and very volatile. And ..." she added, "she doesn't come here very often, there has to be a reason."

They moved forward slowly, deliberately.

"It's the Lady in White. Though she is fabulously beautiful, she is lethal, possessive and eerie. She appears to be human but has the features of a fairy, a dainty, cherry-like mouth, a tiny waist and small feet."

They drew slowly near her and Thena noticed a large wolf with dark fur sitting near her.

"She doesn't look dangerous," said Thena.

"Don't be deceived. She's a shape shifter, like her companion. And if she detects that you're not dead, she might want to eat you."

Thena shuddered.

"She looks like she's sleeping."

"As I said, don't be fooled. The wolf will alert her when we get close enough. She never goes anywhere without her companion."

And Persephone was right. When they were fifty yards from the Woman in White, the wolf suddenly stretched and turned into a demon maid dressed all in gray, who whispered something in the other's ear.

The woman raised her hand and waved Thena and Persephone towards her.

"Come Athena," she began. "Come here to me. Let me look at you. I understand you too are beautiful."

Thena sent a questioning look at Persephone, who with wide eyes and raised brows, nodded her on towards the Woman in White.

Thena moved forward hesitantly and finally stood only a few feet from the woman.

"You are stunning," she said after a few moments examining her, "just as your father predicted."

"My father?" questioned Thena shocked. "You knew my father?"

"Oh yes," she cooed … "quite well in fact."

"How?" asked Thena.

"Unimportant really. All that is important is, that I owe him a debt, as he did an immense favor for me once. It is that debt I intend to repay now," she replied with a slight bow of her head.

Thena's head was spinning. Her father knew this fairy woman! How? She wondered. And what favor could he have done to be owed a debt?

"I know what your mission is …"

"How?" gasped Thena.

"I'm a fay," she started with a little laugh. "We have eyes and ears everywhere." Her eyes gleamed with excitement.

Persephone leaned over and whispered to Thena, "she can read your mind."

"Can I believe her?" Thena whispered back.

Persephone turned to face Thena and shrugged. "Well," she began. "If she meant to harm you, she could have already done it."

"So," began the Woman in White once more. "I have a gift for you."

"Oh!" exclaimed Thena.

"Here, take this!" She handed Thena a dried piece of a plant. It was both hard stemmed and hard leaved. And on it were white berries.

Thena took it, totally unaware of what good it could do but reluctant to offend the woman Persephone had described as lethal, possessive, and eerie.

"What is this?" Thena asked after a moment of hesitation.

"Good girl," remarked the Woman in White. "You did exactly what you should have done … asked. It's moly," she explained with a broad smile, "and it will do what you need it to."

Thena tucked it into the pocket of her pants.

"Now," said the woman, "you need to get on with your task. Uriel has entered the painting. He is looking for you!"

Thena thanked her, and she and Persephone started again along the road beside the river.

A short distance down the road and against the advice of her companion, Thena glanced behind her at the bank where they had left the woman and the wolf. A large white Python now caressed the wolf.

Michael took a few last strokes and glided to the beach. He was tired. The current was much stronger than he thought it would be. But the sun was still out and he knew an hour or so under its rays would dry him out and restore his energy.

The rays were hot, the breeze was gentle and a puzzling aroma filled the air. His eyes felt heavy and soon he nodded off.

When he woke some time later, the sun was just a few degrees above the horizon and he was terribly hungry.

He stood, felt his clothes, which were nearly dry, and checked to be sure he hadn't lost his sword or pack. Then he turned towards the row of palms that lined the beach and surveyed their curve to the right and to the left.

To the right the beach eventually gave way to an outcropping of what in the dimming light appeared to be granite, not the color of fire Michael would expect to see in the waning sunlight. Where there was shade because of the cliffs, shadows too dark to see if they hid caves, made it impossible to tell if going in that direction would be profitable.

So, he turned away and headed for the tree line. The brush was thick ahead and that then gave way to a tropical forest.

He heard a piercing cry, probably a bird, and then an unfamiliar roar of some kind of animal, probably not lions or tigers.

Darkness was gathering and he noticed his hunger cramps worsening. So, he grabbed a handful of red berries from a small tree that reminded him of a Hawthorne and tried one. It was fairly bland, not bitter which would have made him suspect poison, and left no irritation on his lips. Taking the risk, he ate them.

He drew his sword and reluctantly hacked at some underbrush to clear a path.

About a half mile into the trees, the brush thinned and the trees were different. They were shorter, thorny, and had a marked grey bark. On the limbs were some pinkish red fruit that looked a little like apples. He paused long enough to pick several, which he stuffed into his pockets. He bit into one. It was sweet and minty.

The sky had been darkening though there was a bright layer of gold over the ocean behind him, and the wind had begun to build. The leaves on the trees trembled and played a concert on foreign instruments.

He hurried along.

The wind began to gust. Eventually the trees gave way to a grassy meadow and ahead he saw a building that looked like adobe. It shifted color from bright reddish brown to umber. Its walls were broken but he could see at least part of a roof on it. He began to trot. The wind tore at his shirt and pants. The sky was filled with clouds hurrying along like black cars on a busy street.

A shaft of lightning cut the sky, and another. It was followed by deep-throated thunder.

The rain hit him about 100 yards from the wall of the building standing like a broken tooth in gathering darkness. The wind gusted and drove him sideways.

He composed himself, ran and jumped the wall. Inside were bricks scattered randomly by the elements. The roof was partially gone and rain poured down. Ahead, under the covered part of the building he spotted a room and headed for it.

He was shivering when he made it inside. The room was closed in. Its front had heavy iron bars on it. There was a door that banged loudly and randomly against the bars as the rain and wind whipped through.

He made it to the most secure corner, and noticed wood piled along the wall and an ash pit at its base.

He quickly put down his sword and his pack. He grabbed some wood from the wall and laid it in the pit along with some twigs. He found his matches stashed in a pocket and lit a fire. The wood was dry and soon burning merrily. He built a teepee of larger pieces of wood over the small fire and blew gently into the flames.

When the fire was burning steadily and he was warming his hands over it, he settled back against the wall to nap. Suddenly Michael heard the iron gate slam shut and the soft sound of laughter.

He rose swiftly and went to it. It was locked. He tried several times to force it open, each unsuccessful.

Then like a whisper on the wind he heard, "only one left. We'll find her!"

Thena climbed the ancient, stone stairs that led to the upper world. The Taenarus passage was narrow, long and dark.

Persephone had bid her goodbye with a hug, the comment that she had given her a new life and that the old Athena Thompkins was dead. She gave Thena a piece of dark glass on a chain that would cast three spells for her and guaranteed it would be of value later.

She finally made it to the cave that gave the passage its name and after examining it carefully stepped outside.

She stood on a cliff looking over a vast ocean. The wind was gentle and warm. The ground was rocky but large cacti dotted the terrain. It reminded her of a place she loved to visit, Baja. There was a rocky road to her right leading south and the sun stood almost directly overhead.

Instinctively, she knew she had to follow the road. She felt very different than she did before, stronger, more confident and less afraid.

Thena was able to read Lucifer's signature and knew that he had been here. The trail was faint, but she could not tell how long ago it had been.

Lucifer's microbiome would tell her which way to go. She chuckled to herself; she had become very much like a hound. As she walked, she was simultaneously aware that the leather on Lucifer's

Book also had a faint microbiome and that there was danger around her. Lucifer had apparently tried to discourage access to the book by surrounding its path with obstacles all bent to his will.

The road, dusty, rocky and hard-packed, rose ahead, splitting a pair of cacti. She could not see what lay beyond the slope ahead so, she was unprepared when she crested the rise and found two Komodo-sized lizards tearing at the carcass of a gazelle.

At being disturbed, the nearest, a brown and white skinned beast, turned toward her, hissed, and with no further warning lunged.

The beast snapped at her left arm, catching the fleshy part below the elbow and ripping it. The wound was deep and the blood flowed freely. She felt a burning sensation at the bite, then a tingling up her arm. She was suddenly nauseous and dizzy, and she knew she had been poisoned.

Though instantly weak, she managed to stagger away from the lizards, off the side of the road, and into the high desert. Then she passed out.

Twilight was coming on when she woke. Surprisingly, she felt very good. Her head had cleared, and the dragon bite had virtually healed. Only the faintest echo of a scar remained.

She felt very lucky the dragons had not pursued her. She made her way back to where they had been, to continue down the road. They were still there, both bloated and snoring. As she got closer, something caught her eye. The antelope had a large horn in the center of its head.

The horn was fairly thick, very sturdy and curved slightly. It would make a fine weapon, she thought. She carefully stepped over the dragon who had wounded her and began quietly twisting the horn from the skull.

In just a few minutes it pulled free. The lizards, sated, had fallen into a deep slumber but she still moved quietly away before cleaning off the remaining flesh with a handkerchief from her pack.

With the dragons behind her, she continued down the face of the hill to a low marshy plain full of reeds. The footing was wet and difficult but the antelope horn also made a fine walking stick and helped her keep her balance. Every few moments eel-like creatures slithered out of the bog ahead of her, and hissed at her but seemed reluctant to do more.

The wet swampy terrain gradually gave way to a flat grassy plain and then to a steep rise. The journey seemed to go on endlessly and she was feeling fatigue but at the same time she felt herself changing. The steep climb was marked by falling snow, gentle at first and then moderate. Gradually she became aware that her progress was being tracked by large canine creatures, and she could "hear" them speaking.

"Is she the one?" one of the lesser wolves asked.

"Yes," came the answer.

"The master wants us to stop her?" asked another.

"Yes," answered the wolf whom she quickly named "The One," as it seemed to be in charge. "But I don't think we can. Nor do I think it would be in our best interests."

So, they paced her, always keeping their distance behind and to the sides of her. And when a large, green dragon, almost invisible in the falling snow, soared down and challenged Thena. The wolves ran ahead, snarled and nipped at it until it flew off. When she became tired and sat down on a fallen limb, and fell asleep, they not only stood watch, but nestled close to her to keep her warm.

When she woke, they followed her until the snow lessened and the land sloped down to an inlet where fog boiled up from an open stretch of water.

At the shore, there was a gondola-like boat. She stepped into it, grabbed the oars and began to row.

Fog formed itself around her into monstrous, ever-changing shapes that snapped at her. But she was able to vanquish it with a glare and a snap of her fingers.

Persephone was right. She was becoming a different person. She could feel the changes

The boat dipped and moved quicker in an increasingly faster current. Suddenly it was falling. Thena fell out, and found herself in a maze of caverns. She swam, feeling her way intuitively and found herself on the edge of a large, slow moving eddy.

She tried to swim out of it but the tow was becoming greater and greater. And she suddenly knew in a flash of awareness that she should let it take her. She could sense *The Book* she was looking for was at the bottom.

So, she let the whirlpool slowly pull her down and as she was spinning towards the center, she noticed that a glass funnel sat under the surface where she was being dragged. As the force continued to haul her down the funnel, she noticed terrified faces from thousands of years pressed against the glass looking in on her. She could guess from their clothes how long they had been there.

At the bottom, which was basalt, was a glass chamber in which she could see a modern, leather briefcase. She opened the glass chamber and tried to unzip the case. It was locked.

She studied it carefully for several seconds. Finally, she noticed a small microphone built into the handle. She switched it on and began to recite all the names for Lucifer she could remember, beginning with "Lucifer." Then, Abaddon, Beelzebub, devil, Mammon, Satan … until she ran out of names. Nothing happened. She began saying phrases that applied to him: fallen angel, prince of darkness, great dragon, evil one, tempter …. Again, nothing happened.

Of course, she began to think, he did not see himself in a negative way. Rather, he saw himself positively. So, she started again: Angel, beautiful one, favored son, rebel, and for the third time, nothing.

She thought through the mythic story of a war in Heaven, turning it over and over in her mind.

It seemed to her that the key was how Lucifer thought of himself … certainly not in negative way … not as a force of evil but rather as a force of progress, as a force of good, of light.

"Prince of Light," she said. Nothing happened. Then almost in a whisper as thoughts of The Dark Ages and the Renaissance ran through her mind, "Lord of Light!" Of course, Lucifer meant light.

A second later, she heard a click and the briefcase sprang open.

Inside was a book, nearly as large as the case itself, with a red, leather cover and a large image of a horned being in silver leaf.

She touched it hesitantly, running her right index finger slowly up and down the leather and then over the image.

A few minutes later she gathered it up, put a small thumbnail mark in the spine of the new book, and placed it in her bag with the fake one. Then, she closed the briefcase.

She had a plan.

The way back was faster. She felt stronger and discovered that she had abilities she never dreamed of.

The wolves were waiting for her when she returned to the snowy area. The wolf she named "The One" greeted her with a bow and she could read his thoughts. "We will protect you," he sent. She smiled a "Thank you" at him.

Other creatures also moved out of her way.

"Why are they not snapping at me?" she projected.

"Because you have changed. You are not who you were," answered The One.

"How so?"

"You have realized some of your powers. And," he added, "they are ... what is the right word ... more than could be expected. No creature will challenge you now... only the most powerful of the most powerful."

He bowed again when they reached the edge of the wolves' territory and parted ways.

The rest of the journey was without incident. Creatures approached her but turned away on their own.

She wondered about it, but other matters crowded into her thinking. She was satisfied with her plan, but it required some bluffing, some luck and perfect timing.

She saw neither the Woman in White nor Persephone on her way to the ruined building that Persephone had called the House of Ghosts. She did not know how long she would have to wait but she knew what she had to do. After a time, the desperate faces pressing against the glass of the mirrors began to bother her. There was no escaping the faces, the mirrors made up the entirety of the interior walls in the building. Some were young, some were old … all, she thought, were asking her to help them, but she could not hear them, she could not even pick up their projected thoughts as she could with the wolves.

They were, she remembered Persephone telling her, there because of some excess of hubris. Pride had brought them here. She couldn't imagine what any one of them could have done to earn this kind of punishment. She watched a heavily rouged woman with a powdered wig, reddened lips apart, a tight bodice dress get rudely pushed away by a toothless hobo. She'd seen several such incidents since she arrived.

A few hours later, she heard a whisper. It seemed to be coming from them.

"He's coming," came a thought. "He will punish us more."

"No, no, no, you silly woman," came a second comment. "It isn't the master, it's one of his companions."

She was suddenly alert. She knew what she needed to do. She opened the bookbag and took out the volume Michael had given her. She checked the spine to be certain it wasn't the volume she had just retrieved. Thena sat down on the floor with her knees tucked up to her chest and the book, tucked tightly in the crevasse between her chest and knees. The new volume secured in her bookbag.

Her breathing was fast and shallow as she heard him approaching. Her hands were clammy and she was sweating.

He was not quiet. His demeanor didn't allow him to consider failure, no defeat by the creatures he might encounter here.

There was a mighty laugh, then a mocking "Fee fi fo fum." And another laugh. "I always liked that nursery rhyme," he yelled.

Thena didn't respond.

"Are you there little girl?" Uriel shouted.

She didn't answer.

When he entered, Thena saw he was very large, at least eight feet tall and muscular, a shape he had no doubt chosen to intimidate her. And he was a hideous green color, some shade of olive.

As she watched, he transformed his way through the rainbow: orange, red, violet, blue, purple and many shades in between.

Was this really for her benefit? She wondered. Was there some reason why he felt he needed to impress her with his power? Could he sense that she also had powers, like the creatures of this realm? Or was he just a show off? Maybe he's hiding something? Had he heard why many of the creatures who could have easily stopped her refused? Thena's mind was racing.

"Well," he began, "you succeeded in retrieving Lucifer's *Book*. Well done. I didn't expect you, the least of the group, to succeed."

She looked down from the ugly orange color he had settled on, to the floor. Part of her plan was to pretend to cower and look timid.

"I was lucky," she said quietly.

He smiled down at her. "You know, I admire your efforts. You should know that none of the others are going to come rescue you. This is not a movie. This is real life."

He switched suddenly to human size, human color and glared down at her. "They're all out-of-commission!"

"How did you know I got the *Book*?" she asked quietly.

"I have eyes everywhere. They told me. Even if they didn't stop you, they saw your progress. With Lucifer gone, they've picked new allegiances."

"So, if I give you the book, what happens to me?" she asked.

He laughed slightly, a laugh to show his control, to show her that she had no hope.

"Okay," she said solemnly. She untucked her legs and revealed the book. She hesitantly picked it up.

His eyes, wide with greed, followed her.

Thena stood, took it in both hands and threw it against the far wall where covetous faces watched what was happening.

Uriel laughed. "That won't buy you any more time to escape."

He bent down to pick it up, there was a whooshing sound, and he and the book disappeared into the mirror!

She chuckled to herself, very pleased.

———◦((◦))◦———

They had moved on since their encounter with Uriel.

And she eventually found them at Caramel-by-the-Sea in a rented house that overlooked the Pacific.

Fox answered the door when she rang and greeted her with a hug. Wolf and Merlin were having a late afternoon gin and tonic on the deck.

Fox led Thena outside and she settled into a red padded chair.

Thena shook her head yes when Fox asked her if she wanted a drink.

"Are the others dead?" asked Wolf.

"Did you get the *Book*?" asked Merlin.

"One question at a time," said Thena a bit exasperated.

Fox reappeared with a drink in each hand, sat down in an empty, yellow chair, and handed one to Thena.

"And what happened to Uriel?" asked Fox. "Did he get the *Book* from you?"

"Well," started Thena, she took a sip of the Tanqueray and tonic, "I'll give you all some quick answers first and them go back and answer the questions they'll surely generate."

They all nodded their heads in unison. And Thena began.

"I think the others are alive but trapped in Goya's *Mad Carnival* painting. I looked for them but in spite of my newly developed powers, couldn't find them."

Merlin was frowning as she sighed and took another drink.

"I have the other *Book* here, the real one." She patted the bookbag she had been carrying. "Maybe we can use it somehow to find the others and release them." She looked over at Merlin. "You're the most qualified to see if that will work."

He nodded.

"Uriel fell victim to his greed." She explained how she had tricked him in the House of Ghosts.

"So," began Fox as Thena paused for another sip, "he's trapped inside some mirror maze looking at his own self forever?"

Thena shrugged. "That seems like a good guess. But I don't really know. Maybe there's a way out, like there is at a fun house. Maybe not. I saw faces pressed against the glass … desperate people, centuries old, I could tell by their clothes, who hadn't found a way out yet."

Fox had broken into a broad smile. "I love it! It's so ironically appropriate." She started laughing and put her hand over Thena's. "You did great" she said, "just great. You outwitted him."

"It doesn't mean he won't be back," cautioned Wolf.

"True," agreed Merlin. "The fallen have an incredible number of resources, and after being freed of many rules, they even developed them further then when they were in good graces."

"So," Fox began, "let me sum it up."

The others nodded in agreement.

"Uriel is gone … at least for now and we have the real *Book*. But our friends are still trapped somewhere in the Goya and we need to get them out."

"The longer we wait, the more likely they are to be injured or killed," said Thena.

"What do we do?" asked Wolf.

"Well, we have the *Book* and we have Merlin." She nodded towards him.

"True," he agreed.

"If the answer is in the *Book* then Merlin is the most qualified to figure it out."

Thena handed it to Merlin, "I leave the solution in your hands … no pun intended," she added. "Look through it. See if there is anything to help us."

"But you've got to be quick," said Fox.

"Okay," he said, taking the book. "Let me read. In fact, why don't the three of you go up to the Mission Ranch Restaurant and have dinner. Their pulled pork and ribs are superb. Give me some time to study it."

"Good idea," said Wolf.

"Just bring me back a sandwich," added Merlin.

The three of them went to the restaurant and ate. Thena hoped they might see Clint Eastwood or his current girlfriend, but no such luck. Her attention, turned back to finding and rescuing their friends still imprisoned in the painting.

"Where is Le Fay?" asked Thena at one point. "Maybe she can help?" Then without waiting for a response added, "would she be willing?"

"The last I heard," said Fox, "she was in Ft. Collins learning to be a white witch … with that friend of yours … what's her name? Raven?"

"Really?" said Thena, somewhat surprised. "That doesn't sound like her."

"No, it doesn't," replied Fox. "I'm suspicious. I've talked to her a few times by phone and she sounds sincere. But I know her history. Like the others, she'll be after the *Book* or the Elements."

"Don't you trust your sister?" asked Thena.

"Not much," replied Fox. "To become good would be different for her, life altering ...," she quickly corrected herself "... not that she is really evil. She just likes to go her own way."

Wolf and Thena nodded.

"So," began Thena, "there's really no way of knowing if she'll help."

Fox also nodded.

"Do you think Merlin will find anything?" asked Wolf.

"I don't know" responded Fox. "Without the intimidation and manipulation of Nin, he's been a different person. When Uriel fired a bolt of energy at him, he did the fastest shift I've ever seen ... but it wasn't just shifting his body away ..."

"It was a location displacement," said Wolf. "I've only heard about that ability ... never seen it before. Don't know where he went ... but Uriel must have thought he did him in. It was pretty cool," he added with an appreciative smile.

"Interesting," mused Thena.

"Do you think I should ask Morgan for help?" asked Fox, suddenly raising the subject again.

"Why not," said Thena with a shrug. "She can only say no. Why wouldn't she?"

Fox sighed. "She's very suspicious by nature and if she's concocting some grand scheme, she might be happier if Pico and Nin were out of the picture."

"We'd better get going," interrupted Wolf.

<hr>

Merlin was frowning when they got back to the house.

"The pulled pork was delicious," said Fox with a smile as she handed him a take-out container with a sandwich in it.

Wolf brought him a glass of Merlot.

"You don't look happy," remarked Thena, studying his face carefully. "Didn't you find anything to help us?"

Suddenly, his face got even more grave and he shook his head no.

"I'll keep looking," he began. "But …" he stopped and sighed deeply.

"But what?" snapped Fox.

"But none of the spells I tried worked. I'm afraid this *Book*, like the one Michael had, is another fake."

"What!" said Thena.

No one else spoke.

Then, Merlin said, "I've tried every trick I know. But nothing."

They just stared at one another, not believing.